The Highwayman's Cave

THE HIGHWAYMAN'S CAVE

The Fantastic and Romantic Adventures of a Shropshire Legend

NEIL TISDALE

AuthorHouse™
1663 Liberty Drive
Bloomington, IN 47403
www.authorhouse.com
Phone: 1-800-839-8640

© 2012 by Neil Tisdale. All rights reserved.

No part of this book may be reproduced, stored in a retrieval system, or transmitted by any means without the written permission of the author.

Published by AuthorHouse   04/27/2012

ISBN: 978-1-4678-9681-8 (sc)
ISBN: 978-1-4678-9680-1 (e)

Any people depicted in stock imagery provided by Thinkstock are models, and such images are being used for illustrative purposes only.
Certain stock imagery © Thinkstock.

This book is printed on acid-free paper.

Because of the dynamic nature of the Internet, any web addresses or links contained in this book may have changed since publication and may no longer be valid. The views expressed in this work are solely those of the author and do not necessarily reflect the views of the publisher, and the publisher hereby disclaims any responsibility for them.

Contents

Foreword vii

Chapter One 1
Chapter Two 14
Chapter Three 25
Chapter Four 32
Chapter Five 47
Chapter Six 62
Chapter Seven 80
Chapter Eight 88
Chapter Nine 108
Chapter Ten 115
Chapter Eleven 124
Chapter Twelve 139

Foreword

I FIRST CAME across the legend of Wild Humphrey Kynaston and his cave, when I was a child. My grandmother's family home had been near the village of Nesscliffe, above which the sandstone escarpment and cave stand. At school I was always interested in history, in fact going on to study this at university. I decided to take a year out before going to university after finishing my 'A' levels, now usually called a 'Gap' year. During this time I indulged my interest in local history by going to the county reference library in Shrewsbury and reading up on the local folklore.

I came across various documents relating to Humphrey Kynaston, the notorious highwayman of the fifteenth and sixteenth centuries, who had acquired a reputation for both fantastic feats but also generosity and kindness to the poor. I came across documents relating to him being 'outlawed', which I later took as the starting point for the story.

In terms of historical fact Humphrey Kynaston was the youngest son of Sir Roger Kynaston, who had been the High Sheriff of Shropshire. Humphrey was born in 1468, was known to have had 2 wives and died in 1534. He had 2 children from his first marriage and 6 children from his second marriage. He was outlawed first in 1491 and is reputed to have lived in the cave above the village of Nesscliffe. This cave is still there today. It is set into a sandstone escarpment. It has a set of well-defined steps leading up to it. It has a doorway and window space carved from the rock. For the past few years it has not been possible to enter the cave due to health and safety concerns and it is fenced off.

Humphrey is known to have travelled under Henry the Eighth in 1513 to take part in the campaign against France. These are the bare bones of the history. Other than this there were many legends of his daring deeds and those of his equally infamous horse. It is these that I have merged together to try to create a story, mainly fictitious but with a sound basis in history and legend.

I must give acknowledgement to the book published in 1899 by Henry Hudson entitled 'Wild Humphrey Kynaston—The Robber Troglodyte: A romance of the Robin Hood of Shropshire in the reign of Henry the Seventh.'

I read this book which had clearly covered the same subject matter. But I felt that the character of Humphrey Kynaston could do with a more modern interpretation. Reading about him I tried to imagine what sort of man he was, why did he become an outlaw? How did he get this reputation of giving to the poor? He appeared to me to be a rebel to the life-style that he had been born into and slowly I began to create the character in my mind.

It has taken me many years to get around to putting flesh to the bones that I created then. Hopefully this has been due to having a busy life with lots of other distractions. Now I would like to give the character the chance to come to life and give entertainment to many people again, as I am sure he did during his own life-time.

I would like this book to be dedicated to my good friend Jim, who I have known since meeting him at York University in 1975. He died tragically in November 2011. He was a great lover of art, ceramics, history and literature and I hope that he might have appreciated my effort.

For JIM

Chapter One

The Sheriff's man rode slowly and warily along the muddy and stony track. Alone, he had good reason to feel apprehensive. Even his horse seemed to be aware of the pervading atmosphere, as it stumbled along, its ears twitching nervously and its eyes flashing from one to the other of the ragged men standing either side of the track. She seemed ready to make a dash for safety, were there to be any suspicious move from this ragged and hoary band.

The men, mostly dirty, unshaven, many with scars or other abominable features, simply stood or sat staring at the smart figure on his smart horse. They were silent except for a few murmurs of suspicion. To the horseman it seemed a threatening silence. He noted the knives and swords hanging from the ruffians' waists and rested his hand on his own sword in anticipation.

He passed under the sign where a wolf's head snarled ferociously down at him and he involuntarily jerked his head away. The men seemed to be snarling at him also. The horseman reined up outside the inn door and gingerly leaving the hilt of his sword pulled from his saddlebag a notice. Without dismounting for fear of assault he leaned across to the doorpost and nailed up the notice. His duty done he turned his horse around and trotted off back down the track. Reaching a bend a few hundred yards away he halted to breath a sigh of relief. He looked back seeing the men at the inn hustling around the notice he had just posted. The relieved deputy then rode on out of sight and into safety.

"Wots it say?" growled some husky voices.

"Read it out!" demanded another.

They had all crowded around the notice on the inn door, eager to know its meaning. They were not used to a Sheriff's man riding into the area let alone to come into their midst and post a public notice. They had been all too startled to begin with, when he first rode in, to do anything about it. This was perhaps the only thing which had saved the young deputy, whose anxiety had been by no means unjustified. This was the 'Wolf's Head Inn' notorious around the county. All sorts of ruffians, robbers and outlaws could be seen here, and usually smelt as well, such was the state of the place. Anybody would be lucky to come out of there without his money gone or his throat slit, let alone a representative of the sheriff and the magistrates.

"Come on! Read the blasted thing out!" bellowed a voice from the back of the small crowd. It emanated from a big figure, broad as well. What should have been a head was covered with a mass of black fuzz and only some small narrow slits could be seen where normally there are eyes.

"If yer inner gonner read it, get someone else!" came the voice again and the bear-like figure pushed and jostled towards the front, as were some others trying to do. Curses and oaths were thrown at one another as the ragged mob grew impatient and as people were knocked aside or trodden on as each tried to see what the notice said. But as none could read, nothing happened until someone fetched the landlord to read it out.

"Come on Bill, tell us wot it say!"

"Ar, an' urry it up" and other such exclamations were shouted out, as all were eager and impatient to know the meaning of the notice.

"Alright, settle yer damn selves down, now. Or I wanner read it." Shouted out the semi Welsh tones of the landlord. The din slowly subsided with still a few muffled comments and murmurs from the crowd.

"Now let me see" began the landlord, himself a big man and probably needed to be as well. He was slightly better dressed than his customers, but only slightly and with his hairless, even clean shaven face and his rotund body he looked a genial man, certainly not suited to his occupation and clientele. But his appearance was deceiving and purposely so. Underneath this façade he was probably even more ruthless and cut-throat than many of the men he served, as many had already learned to their demise. To the militia, whenever they paid him a visit, he could put on the picture of perfect innocence while at the same time concealing some wanted outlaw or some stolen property. Although they did not believe a word that he said neither the militia nor the magistrates had been able to prove anything against him. Even if they had done, they would need more than proof to take him or any of his friends from this thieves haven. The magistrates knew this only too well which fact added to the bewilderment of the outlaws and to the probable importance of the mission when the lone deputy had been sent in to put up the official notice.

"Well, it reads something like this" continued the landlord after a few moments of consideration.

> "IN THE NAME OF HENRY BY THE GRACE OF GOD KING OF ENG ..."

"Oh, just get on with it, come on." various growling voices interrupted.

"Oh, alright. Hold your tongues or it wanner be read." The landlord started again as the crowd quietened down once more.

> "THE MAGISTRATES OF SALOP DO HEREBY GIVE NOTICE OF THE INDICTMENT OF MURDER TO BE SERVED ON ONE HUMPHREY KYNASTON WITH ACCOMPLICES ONE THOMAS KYNASTON AND ONE ROBERT HOPTON, WHO DID ON TUESDAY NEXT BEFORE THE FEAST OF CHRISTMAS FELONIOUSLY AND BARBAROUSLY RIDE DOWN ONE JOHN

HUGHES OF STRETTON IN THAT SAID PLACE, WHO DID DIE OF THE WOUNDS THUS INFLICTED. THE AFORESAID HUMPHREY KYNASTON, LATE OF NESSCLIFFE, LATE OF KNOCKYN AND MYDDLE CASTLES IN THE MARCHES OF WALES, SON OF ROGER KYNASTON OF HORDLEY IS THUS INDICTED AND OUTLAWED. IT IS THE DUTY OF EVERY CITIZEN OF THIS COUNTY OF SALOP WHO DOES KNOW ANYTHING OF THE FORESAID HUMPHREY KYNASTON OR HIS ACCOMPLICES TO DISCLOSE ANY SUCH KNOWLEDGE TO THE MAGISTRATES OF THE SAID COUNTY ON PAIN OF IMPRISONMENT."

The crowd were for a few moments deadly silent, and then a subdued murmur began spreading through the crowd. Each ruffian looked knowingly and ominously at his neighbour. Few words were needed as all had the same thoughts in their heads.

"I knew he'd do it one o' these days. I always said so" murmured one of mob.

"Ar, he always was a rum un, but he's gone too far this time." Said another and other comments and mutterings generally of agreement came from every other part of the crowd. A stranger could make little of their mutterings but each man of this mob knew the story only too well. They had seen the same happen to so many other men, including themselves but never before to someone of such class. The Humphrey Kynaston mentioned in the notice had often been a customer at this inn, had drunken much and gambled to such an extent that already he was known as 'Humphrey the Wild' around this locality. He was known to be in debt to many people and his behaviour was getting more riotous and dissolute until now he had made the final riotous step into outlawry. This was the common story of many men in these parts but the customers of the 'Wolf's Head Inn' could not help but be a little surprised that a man of such gentile descent should join their throng. The bear-like figure at the back of the crowd stood sullen and slightly apart from the rest. What little of his face could be seen from amongst the fuzz seemed meditative and slightly disturbed.

"Hey Hopton!" someone turned to towards him but there was no response.

"Oi, Hopton" This time he prodded the broad figure.

"What! What yer want?" responded the black beard startled back to life.

"Well, what are yer gonner do? They'll be after yer now, I know."

"That's for certain" agreed Bill the landlord stepping over to join them.

"They'll take it serious this time with Kynaston in with it anall."

"Aw, dunner worry about me, they wanner be after me so much. That feller was already near enough dead afore me an' Tom got to him. It'll be young Kynaston what's gonner take the brunt of it." The bearded Robert Hopton did not look unduly worried about being wanted, it was certainly nothing new for him to be outlawed.

"But all the same" he added, "I'll have to go an' warn Humphrey. They'll want him for sure."

"Ar," mused the landlord, "He's never bin popular with the magistrates, specially as he's one of their kind himself. You'd better go and warn him, they'll soon want to be on his tail."

Already decided Hopton had turned away to the stables leaving the rest of the crowd murmuring and muttering about the recent happenings, some offering various predictions on what might happen but others had already drifted back into the Inn to refill their tankards: The incident was no real concern of theirs, it simply provided another talking point.

In a moment Hopton stepped out of the stables leading his mount, a huge smutty-coloured beast of over 18 hands. He threw himself up onto its back and even this huge beast shuddered for a moment beneath his master's weight. The muscles of both rippled as the pair moved off ponderously up the track, in the opposite direction to that taken by the Sheriffs' man. By now all the men had moved inside the inn and returned to their ale, all that is except for the landlord himself who still stood watching the pair disappear into the misty woodland.

William Thomas, or Bill to his customers was used to harbouring many outlaws but he was a little uncertain about this one. This was something different and he was not sure he could afford to harbour any of this particular group. The militia were bound to come and search his premises and with a person as important as Wild Humphrey Kynaston it would be more than difficult to keep them at bay. It might come to a showdown and with the militia in force Bill could not be sure of coming out best. He stood pondering for another 5 minutes until some impatient customers shook him out of his reverie and he returned to the hustle and bustle of the tavern.

By now Hopton had stirred his mount into a brisk trot, though a heavy trot, and was well on his way to Knockyn where Roger Kynaston, Humphrey's father resided and where Hopton knew Humphrey to be staying. Although the ground was covered in mud as it was at the beginning of the year, the huge horse could still make good time, lifting its feet high above the cold slushy mud and striding knee-deep through ice-cold streams. In only a short while he came in sight of the Kynaston family home, a small stone castle already starting to show signs of the diminishing family fortune, mostly attributable to the younger son's extravagances. Hopton slowed his mount a little wishing to approach with caution, knowing his presence would certainly not be welcomed by the old father, who disapproved of almost everything his son did, especially the company he kept.

Humphrey was son only by second marriage and perhaps it was resentment at this or perhaps a reaction against his father's honourable and upright way of life that had made him turn to his own wild manner of living. His father had been one of the most respected men in the county, had been

The Highwayman's Cave

Sheriff and held many other honourable offices as well as having won great honour and renown on the battlefield during the Wars of the Roses and what is more they were descended from Welsh Princes no less, all of which the father had not been loath to relate to his remiss son. Whatever the reason father and son had never got on well together and as the old father and young Humphrey had both grown older, so the parents hold and control had diminished along with the family fortune, till now the father had grown ill and was confined to the castle. Humphrey, however, roamed freely causing trouble and raising scandal.

Under cover of the oak trees which flourished in this area Hopton was able to approach the outskirts of the castle unnoticed. Here with great effort he dismounted and tied his mount to a nearby tree. From here he crept as stealthily as could a man of his size and eventually still unnoticed he reached the main buildings where he began looking for his young companion in crime. He found no trouble in entering the gates, there being no need for a guard at the castle of such a renowned hero and he strode up to the main house. Still not sure how his presence would be greeted he preferred not to make a direct entry but instead he crept around the building hoping to see Humphrey alone through a window. Having passed a number of windows he suddenly halted. From the next room along he could hear a heated argument and one of the voices he recognised as that of Humphrey. He moved slowly forward and peered through a corner of the large window. In a splendid, ornate room stood leaning across a large oak-wood table Hopton could see a tall distinguished old man with long grey hair and beard but his normal pallid features seemed flushed. He stood quivering and shouting across the room at the back of another man. All he could see of the other man was that he had long jet-black hair and was dressed in riding clothes. Suddenly he turned around to face the older man, provoked by something the elder had said and for the first time his full features could be seen. He was a young man in his early twenties with sharp handsome features, small brown eyes, normally twinkling, now glared across at his opposite figure. He was tall and slim but still of good build and dangling aside his long black boots hung a sword, not easily overlooked. Hopton immediately recognised this as his wild young companion. Not wanting to show himself in front of the father, whom he guessed the irate grey-haired gentleman to be, he remained concealed but listened attentively.

"I shall never permit a murderer to reside beneath my roof" screamed the parent, "You have dragged our ancestral name through the mud for long enough. I shall have no more of it. I shall not. I shall not." His voice almost reached hysteria as he screeched at his outlawed son.

"Have you no respect for the honour of your family? How could I ever have had a son like you, myself a late Sheriff of this very county? I shall harbour you no longer."

"Do not worry yourself, Sir; I have no intention of remaining here. I simply returned here for my property. I shall leave immediately." Roared out the young man with not a little contempt as well.

"Property! Are not your wife and family property? But of course you shall not take them with you. Do you care for none but yourself?"

"You know my opinions on that subject" retorted Humphrey defiantly, "She was not of my choosing. The marriage was of your organisation. I do not feel bound by any such arrangement."

"Then we have nothing left to discuss. I will have no more to do with you. Leave here immediately and never return to sully our name again!" With this the old man, still shaking and trembling with rage, turned his back on his son. Humphrey without another word strode out. Humphrey did not see, but Hopton did, as he remained concealed at the window, the dignified old man collapse into the big arm-chair still shaking but his face suddenly turned a deadly pale and was gasping for breath.

Hopton turned away unconcerned and went to meet his companion, who now strode from the house.

"'umphrey!" he growled. Kynaston turned, a little surprised but the anger and defiance still flushing his face. "Yer've gotta get away quick, 'umphrey. They've posted on yer this morning and they'll be after yer soon."

"Don't worry Robert. I am already going into hiding. I have already made plans. But what about you? They will be after you too." Came the self-confident reply.

"Ah, dunner worry about me neither. There's many a place I can hide out an' they wanner bother with me too much. It's you they want."

"Well, you had better be off from here before my father sees you. He has never been particularly inclined towards outlaws, not even when his own son is numbered amongst them." Suggested the young man, now calmer than before.

"Ar, yer right enough there. I'll be going." With that and a nod of farewell Hopton slouched back across the yard and through the gates, his bear-like figure for a moment framed against the sky by the pillars before disappearing around the corner.

Humphrey was already at the stable door before Hopton had disappeared, he was in no mood for wasting time. He never liked doing so at all but especially at a time like this. He walked along the stables past 4 or 5 horses till he came to the one he was looking for. He halted at the rear of a large brown mare, but so dark a brown that to some it looked black. He patted her on the rump and she turned her head knowingly. Her ears were pricked and she watched her master attentively with sharp energetic eyes. Kynaston moved up to her head and stroked her and whispered into her soft brown ears. She pushed her head fondly against his chest and in the darkness of the stable an affectionate grin could be seen on Kynaston's face. Silently and softly he saddled the mare and then led her out into the courtyard. No further preparations were needed, he had all he needed, his horse and his sword. He swung easily up into the saddle and as he mounted he saw the decrepit figure of his father leaning against the doorpost. He galloped off through the gates and away.

Into the woods he went, at first travelling the same way that Hopton had ridden, but he turned off before he came to the Wolf's Head. He rode around the back of it and further into the woods and higher into the low range of hills behind. It was hard going up the steep hills through the thick mud and along the narrow pathways winding amongst the trees, but the mare was up to the task. The hill became steeper and steeper. After a while he emerged from the undergrowth into a clear space, both horse and rider sweating despite the cold. Now towering above the pair stood the bare sandstone rock. It was almost sheer. Halfway up there was a black shadow. Kynaston dismounted and left his mount at the foot of the cliff. He then scrambled up the steep sandstone face till he reached the dark shadow of the cave and he peered into the darkness, the familiar darkness of his childhood. He had visited this cave and these hills many times as a boy, he knew them almost as well as the back of his hand. He turned around and looked outward over the hamlet of Nesscliffe and further to the Welsh hills from where his own ancestors had reputedly come. But he felt differently than ever he had done before in this cave. He felt apprehensive but also excited as he looked out from his vantage point at what seemed to be the whole world spread at his feet. He felt independent, really free but with the accompanying loneliness and apprehension. With his back to the friendly darkness of the cave he stood not knowing what the future would bring or how long he was destined to stay in exile.

Chapter Two

That had been at the beginning of the year 1492, when only 21 years of age, and now over a decade on Humphrey Kynaston could still be found looking out from his cave over the Welsh hills and his fine mare grazing below. But much had happened in those intervening years. He had been correct in supposing himself safe here, high up in the sandstone cliff. The magistrates and Sheriff had initiated a search but with only small forces at their command and the local peasantry hostile towards them the search had met with little success. In fact none of the three outlaws were captured, neither Hopton who took refuge amongst his fellow thieves, nor Humphrey's elder half-brother Thomas who was hardly bothered by the militia at all. The militia had searched Knockyn castle but were days too late and the cumulative effect of these happenings, his defiant younger son being outlawed and his own age and illness, were that the distinguished old knight, Roger of Hordley, had died not long after. The castle was now inhabited by Humphrey's mother and occasionally his half-brother Thomas.

But all this was nothing compared to the change in life-style this exile had forced on Humphrey himself. An outlaw, he had no option but to survive by felony and his new place of abode facilitated this profession superbly. From his cave, standing high above the surrounding area overlooking Nesscliffe and Kynaston, he could plainly see everybody and everything that travelled the main route from Shrewsbury to Oswestry. It was the only route the rich drapers and clothiers could take to reach the main Welsh flannel market held in Oswestry and whether going or coming they were sure to be weighed down by much wealth. The young quick-witted Kynaston was never a man to waste such an opportunity, so armed with lance or sword and astride his fine steed he had become a highwayman and had been the scourge of this section of road for the past few years.

He was now about to set out on another raid. He had heard of one particular wealthy draper who was travelling with only a few other men on his way to the Oswestry market to purchase some cloth. He now watched attentively for the cart to appear for it would take him and his fleet-footed horse only five or ten minutes to race down to the road and apprehend them on their journey. But as he watched for the draper his eyes could not help but be distracted by the Welsh hills beyond, which every time he saw them seemed to fill him with renewed strength and new blood; the blood of his rebellious and riotous Welsh ancestors which seemed to burn with fire in his veins.

Then plodding around a wide bend a few miles up the road to Shrewsbury appeared the draper's cart. The draper sat beside the driver and there was only one other man mounted on a horse. In a second Kynaston caught sight of them and scrambled down the rough steps which he had carved out during his exile. He whistled for his precious companion who came galloping up to him with a brisk gambol. She nestled her head down to his chest and he stroked her fondly.

"That's my lovely. Come on gal, we have some more business." He spoke softly and reassuringly. The mare pricked up her ears and both man and horse seemed to have the same twinkling in their dark brown eyes. Kynaston swung himself majestically into the saddle and the pair raced away down the hillside, dodging over the rocks and through the trees as if they knew every inch of the route, as indeed they probably did. Under cover of the trees they reached the edge of the main highway still unseen. Here they could wait, for such had been their speed that they had arrived well before the drapers cart was due.

The pair had been on so many such robberies together that the mare knew the procedure almost as well as the highwayman himself. They waited calmly but both had the glow and sheen of nervous perspiration. All was absolutely silent except for the wind rustling the leaves and the heavy breathing of the horse and rider. Although daytime, no birds could be heard in the trees, even they seemed to sense the coming event. It was midday in early spring; it was indeed to be a most daring robbery. The draper had probably thought himself safe from attack travelling at this hour in broad daylight. How little he knew of 'Wild Humphrey Kynaston', as the highwayman was now widely known, who so far had been too sharp for everyone.

Still only the breeze in the leaves could be heard, only thoughts disturbed Humphreys mind. Then his mare pricked up her ears.

"What is it, old gal?" whispered the highwayman quickly, "Can you hear them? Ah, yes, there they are. Just keep calm, gal, till they come."

The wooden cartwheels could be heard rumbling and sloshing along the highway, which was still wet from the recent thaw. The rumbling drew nearer until from his place of hiding Humphrey could see the caravan as it came around another small bend. Two oxen pulled laboriously at the yoke as they trudged through the mud and as the cart approached the highwayman could see that neither the carter nor the draper were armed. But from the waist of the accompanying rider there hung a sword. Kynaston mused upon this for a moment but did not seem unduly worried. Yard by yard the cart approached, then slapping his mare's rump the highwayman started from the bushes and onto the highway. He stood calmly blocking the road and the carter pulled up with a start.

"Good day, master draper. I hope you intended a good day at the market." Said the robber-knight politely. The draper and his companions were frozen in silence.

"I am in a hurry today" continued the robber, "So hand over your purse and let's have no trouble." He stirred his mount and began to move forward to collect his earnings.

"Get him, man!" roared the draper, finally overcoming his shock and the mounted guard drew his short sword and came forward to attack.

"Don't be a fool!" advised the robber, himself reaching for the short lance lying alongside the saddle, but the guard rode on. "Here goes, gal" he shouted to his mare and they raced towards the oncoming guard, who armed only with a sword stood little chance. Kynaston was accurate in his aim and the short lance drove full into the chest of his brave but foolish adversary. He was carried clean from the back of his mount and crashed groaning and bleeding onto the road, where he his blood mixed freely with the brown mud and formed a sickening colour.

"I gave you warning, master draper" said the highwayman coldly as he rode on to the cart. "Now let us have no more playing. I have no time for it."

The draper, scared into obedience, had little choice but to pull out his purse from his waistcoat pocket. Kynaston snatched it eagerly as he came alongside the cart and a wry grin spread across his face as he felt the weight of the purse.

"A handsome purse indeed, this should see me well in ale tonight. Good day again to you, sir." And he rode back into the trees chuckling as he went, leaving the draper hurling curses in every other direction and the prostrate guard still groaning horribly, not quite dead.

Humphrey did not return to his hideout but instead went by a wide detour to another of his local taverns, 'The Three Pigeons.' He felt in a buoyant mood after his fresh success and was in the mood to have some fun. He rode up to the inn, checking first for suspicious circumstances, for he was never so elated not to be cautious. He dismounted and stabled his mare, but he did not unsaddle in case a quick escape might be needed. He strode out of the stable with a bouncing gait and across the yard to the inn. Outside, leaning against the doorpost, sat a blind and semi-crippled beggar, who had been maimed in the same wars that Humphreys father had gained his honour. Humphrey looked into the dead eyes of the old beggar and his step faltered.

"Here you are, old Cedric. Have a drink on me." And he flung a few coins into the beggars hat.

"Yer a fine gen'leman, sir, a fine gen'leman." The old beggar nodded his head in appreciation. Were he only to have been sighted could he really have appreciated the value of the gift, only then could he have seen the rich lustre and shiny gleam, but as it was he could only judge by the feel of the coins and by the amount of food and drink they would provide.

Wild Humphrey walked on into the dark, reeking den of thieves, where he had had so many enjoyable times in these past few years.

"Its Wild Humphrey!" called out various voices from the darkness of the low beamed room. Other greetings and acknowledgements were exchanged with the newcomer.

"Drinks all around, my old friends! No, make it twice over." Roared out Humphrey in celebration of his recent success. Cheers and noises of surprise emanated from the rough mob who now all clambered to their feet and fought their way across the room to refill their tankards.

"An' what do we owe this 'onour, ay? Another windfall?" Shouted someone amidst roars of laughter and a clattering of mugs.

"No, lads" grinned Humphrey, "Just a little business transaction." Laughter again. The men took their free drinks and then returned to whatever they were doing before Humphrey came in, some to drinking and joking, some to dice, others to women and the rest to generally just enjoying themselves. This was the kind of life and company he had always preferred to that strict, stultifying influence of his father, ever since he had been old enough to choose. He had never been able to accept the values of honour, loyalty and chivalry that his father and his friends had always spouted, and what was more he had found that life too dull. His fiery temperament and rich blood could never rest under such restrictions and obligations as his father had tried to impose. This was the life he loved.

He gulped down a tankard of ale and replenished it immediately, feeling the liquor wash away the dirt in his throat and the sight of blood from his mind. He went across to the dice table and joined in, not caring too much whether he came out better or worse, the excitement was the main thing, as with everything else with Wild Humphrey. He also preferred the rough and ready women he could find at these establishments, much more interesting and satisfying to him than the cold, inhibited females of his own class. Perhaps that was the reason he left his wife but perhaps there were other reasons as well.

He lost himself for a time in the ale and amongst the joking and gaming, and he became just another of the drunken ruffians who frequented the inn. He played dice, drank, played with the women, drank and played again. The afternoon passed and soon it began to grow dull outside but this was hardly noticeable from the darkness of the tavern, everyone simply continued drinking and joking.

Later on in the evening Humphrey was called away from the dice-table by a voice at the bar. He could not see who it was till he came almost right against him.

"Ah, Thomas, and where 'av yer bin" slurred out Humphrey, "You're late. Yer've missed all the fun."

"I hear that you have had a little luck this morning." Humphrey simply nodded and grinned in response. "A trifle risky in broad daylight, was it not?"

"Don't worry about me, Thomas, I can 'andle anything anytime" chuckled out Humphrey, slurping back some more ale.

"Well, I am very glad you said that, Humphrey, for I have some news" He beckoned Humphrey into a lone dark corner away from the laughing and the gambling. Humphrey put down his tankard and followed with a curious twinkle in his eye. They sat down and after checking that nobody was listening Thomas began,

"Well, I happened to be in Shrewsbury this morning and I also happened to overhear a conversation concerning the collection of some tenants' arrears."

"This does sound interesting" whispered Humphrey, his mood suddenly changing. "Pray, continue dear brother."

"It will be dangerous as it will again be in daylight but what is more the collection is so close to Shrewsbury itself that the Sheriffs men will never be far away. One could easily ride straight into a military patrol."

"Well, come on. Tell me more. How much? Where? When? Who?" demanded Humphrey growing more and more interested.

"Alright, do not get over excited" said Thomas "I cannot tell how much but it should be a sizeable purse for it is Squire Lloyd who is ordering the collection and you know how large his estates are."

A new steely glint came to Humphreys eyes at this revelation, not at the prospect of great fortune, though this indeed had some effect on him, but because the man he would be robbing would be Squire Lloyd, an old friend of his fathers and consequently an enemy of himself. They had by proxy had many encounters with each other and each was by now the sworn enemy of the other. Such thoughts ran through Humphreys head but he said nothing. Thomas continued,

"Lloyd's man will be collecting from early morning and he should be done by mid afternoon. That would be the best time to take him, but also the most risky."

Both men sat silent, looking at the dark surface of the table between them. It was true, this kind of robbery was more risky than robbing the drapers and clothiers; they had to come this way, miles from the town and past his very lair, but with the rent collectors of the various squires and estates it was necessary to go and find them, sometimes necessitating a long journey back to his safe hideout. Also robbing from the gentry could have more serious consequences, especially from men like Lloyd. They had great influence in the county and many were themselves magistrates and could thus make life very difficult for Kynaston.

"Alright, tell me the details" said Humphrey calmly and businesslike. Thomas then explained where exactly the best place for an ambush would be, an appropriate time and other details of information relating to the planned robbery. The robbing of rent collectors was a new step for Humphrey and it had gained him much fame and acclamation from amongst the peasant farmers and tenants. They saw him as their defender against their masters and oppressors, the men who were squeezing their last hard earned coppers from their pockets. Already people were acclaiming him as their hero, robbing from the rich to give to the poor. Humphrey himself would have none of this; he robbed the rich for his own ends and left the poor alone only because they were poor and not worth robbing, and if he was occasionally generous this was from no moral decision but simply because he wanted to and could afford it. What else could he do with his illegally acquired money anyway? So Humphrey thought.

"Well, I shall be off to Knockyn now. And are you leaving?" asked Thomas.

"No," grinned Humphrey again in a jocular mood, "I think I shall be staying here tonight" and he nodded towards a flirty young woman over at the gaming table, with long, black tresses falling over her bare shoulders, exposed by her loose, low-cut dress. Thomas also grinned.

"Will you need any help tomorrow?" he asked, "Hopton is always ready."

"No, no. You know I prefer to be alone."

"Are you alright for provisions up there? Do you need anything else?"

"No, no" replied Humphrey. He was looking back across the room, no longer interested in what his step-brother was saying. Seeing that the conversation was over and that Humphreys mind was elsewhere, Thomas stood up, took his hat and cloak and with a word of farewell, which went unnoticed, left.

Humphrey had already started walking back to the laughter and he stopped only to pick up another tankard of ale. He rejoined the revelry, the drinking and the joking, and thus passed another few hours till night had well fallen. Then he rose quietly leaving the dicers to haggle and chatter on. He looked askance over his shoulder and beckoned to a figure waiting patiently at the rear of the inn. The figure stood up and the pale moonlight coming through the open door lit up the bare white neck and shoulders. Humphrey walked over to a door at the back of the inn, opened it and went upstairs. The dark figure glided silently across the floor and followed.

CHAPTER THREE

THE MARE GAMBOLLED along, its' staccato taps making a pleasant sound. Soft, young sunlight glistened in the puddle-filled pot-holes of the track. The birds sang energetically amongst the flourishing branches and new, innocent colour could be seen everywhere. Everything was cheerful and the smartly clad rider had every reason to believe that all would go well on his mission ahead. The pair jogged on merrily towards their destination, Kynaston was silent with a static grin on his face. He was really looking forward to today's adventure, especially as it would hurt Squire Lloyd. He rode on along the Nesscliffe road towards Shrewsbury, he was heading for a junction of highways, where this road met the Shrewsbury to Welshpool highway. This is where Thomas had suggested would be the best place of ambush. The junction was only a few miles from Shrewsbury itself, so at this time of day it was indeed a most risky and dangerous exploit. The Sheriffs men were sure to be quickly on his trail and he had a long ride back to safety, but this only added to the challenge and excitement. Humphrey had no apprehensions or fears and rode on boldly and confidently.

He smelled the fresh smell of moisture as the clean sunlight shone refreshingly down. He enjoyed listening to the birds and seeing the fresh blooms on the trees and amongst the bushes. On either side of him stretched strips of land topped by smooth, gentle hillocks covered in the fresh, young green of spring, here and there dotted with the white of sheep. Musing thus on the surrounding country, the country he had always loved and felt part of, it seemed no time at all till he reached his destination.

He had no idea when the rent collector was due, so he looked about for somewhere to rest. A few hundred yards further on he caught sight of a large oak tree, which was wide enough to conceal behind it both horse and rider. He rode over and dismounted. He settled down keeping his ears pricked for any rider, leaving his horse to graze peacefully. He looked at the wide base and the old gnarled bark; he was himself sitting on one of the huge, curved and interwoven roots. He strolled around the huge base. On one side there was a hollow, perhaps just large enough for a man. Humphrey felt the sturdy trunk and thought that this was a fine place to hide. He resumed his wait sitting with the trunk at his back.

To his surprise he did not have to wait long for the very next rider who appeared was the very one Humphrey was seeking. He rode alone and as far as he could see from his hiding place unarmed. Very strange: but all to the advantage. The collector, dressed in a dark grey cloak rode slowly and steadily, certainly in no hurry to return the taxes to his master. Humphrey whistled quietly and his mare raising her head from grazing came quickly to her master. He mounted and waited, pulling a cloth across his face. The rider approached looking about him. Seeing no urgency Humphrey trotted his mare out onto the highway and turned towards the oncoming tax collector.

The collector reined up.

"You should not attempt to escape" calmly advised the dark-clad robber, "I do not think your old beast could outrun my beauty. So let us have no trouble. Hand over your purse!" He rode slowly forward, his hand on the hilt of his sword.

"There's no need for that. I won't fight "replied the collector.

"That is very sensible" said Kynaston taking the fat purse and slipping it into his saddle-bag. "Your master can surely spare it. Tell him I thank him most heartily, when you see him next." He said grinning with every muscle in his face, "Farewell."

He dug his spurs into the side of his mount and away he galloped, and so did the collector in the opposite direction. Kynaston wanted to get away as far as possible before the collector could rouse the Sheriff. Both horse and rider seemed elated which fact seemed to add to their speed. They clattered away down the Nesscliffe road leaving behind them the old oak tree and the scene of the robbery. The hills and the trees flashed by them in one general green blur as they sped on eager to be home. They slowed down a little as ahead of them lay a narrow wooden bridge crossing the fast flowing river, flushed full to bursting by the recent thaw. The mare's hooves clattered on the wooden planks. Suddenly they crashed to a halt, the horse reared and neighed frantically. Kynaston struggled desperately to stay in the saddle. Looking ahead he saw that many of the planks from the middle of the bridge were missing. Below swirled the sickly, mud-coloured surge of the flood, carrying with it trees, branches and other debris being churned up and thrown into the air, as if trying to escape, but only to drop back into the liquid inferno.

Humphrey with difficulty turned his mount around and rode back onto the firm Shropshire earth.

"Thanks, gal. You saved us there." Gasped Humphrey, sweat pouring from his brow. "We shall have to cross further downstream."

But as he started moving again, having regained some composure, from the trees and bushes in front of them emerged a group of armed men. The militia! A trap! Thoughts flashed quickly through his mind.

"Give up Kynaston! We have you surrounded this time. There is no escape." The command came from an ornately dressed gentleman, who Humphrey guessed to be the Sheriff. He rode at the head of about 7 or 8 militia men, with another dozen or so on foot at the rear. The Sheriff was right; there did appear to be no escape.

Humphrey had to think quickly as the men began to close in. Behind him swirled and gurgled the river in full torrent, in front of him stood the Sheriff and his men.

Suddenly he again turned his mare around.

"Come on, gal. It's the only way we can make it." He whispered patting her neck. He dug his spurs into her sides and with a start she galloped fearlessly forward.

"Halt!" called a voice from behind, hardly audible above the swirling and rushing of the torrent below the pair as they reached the bridge. Unfaltering the mare rushed on. The missing planks seemed wider than a chasm as they rode closer. The pair became one as they charged on, the same thoughts flooded into their minds, they became one consciousness. They leaped.

The clattering of hooves on wooden planks told the pair that they were over. They had made it. They charged on till they once again till they reached the firm land, where panting and sweating but relieved they turned defiantly to face their pursuers stranded on the opposite bank.

"Foul luck, Sir. Perhaps you will have better fortune on another occasion." Laughed Humphrey and his horse neighed in agreement. Or relief. They galloped off again leaving their pursuers open-mouthed and pop-eyed, too astonished to curse, staring helplessly after them.

"An' yer know what?"

"No, no, go on mon."

"Ar, carry on" came the responses from the rest.

"Well, as I was a sayin'. He was trapped, yer see, but Wild Humphrey was too quick for 'em. In a flash he had turned around and was away over the gorge"

Murmurs and gasps of amazement emanated from the surrounding group.

"It was all of forty feet or more, I know" the narrator added. Mutterings of 'never', 'surely not' and so on was the response from his audience. But the ragged, old narrator would have none of their scepticism, he confirmed and repeated emphatically his tale.

"I was there, myself, y'know. I was hid in the trees."

The listeners settled down a little. Already stories of Humphrey Kynaston's exploits were spreading from inn to inn throughout this sector of the county. He was now the main talking point every evening in almost every inn within a twenty or thirty mile radius. With his fame grew his popularity, but of course this was only amongst the lower classes for it was only to be expected that he was by no means popular with the gentry or the merchants. Some of Humphrey's exploits grew by rumour and repetition. They reached fantastical limits and others were probably created in the minds of the people, from their imagination and their hope. Stories were spread of his great generosity and kindness towards the poorer people, which only added to his popularity. Before he knew it himself, Wild Humphrey was becoming a legend even while he still lived.

"An' that's not all" continued the old man eagerly, taking another sup from his tankard of ale.

"What d'yer mean?" asked someone.

The old man glanced around quickly each side of him to check that he had the complete attention of his audience. They all leaned towards him in eager anticipation.

He went on,

"Well, seeing that it was a trap, he guessed who was behind it. It was old Squire Lloyd, y'see. So next day Wild 'Umphrey rides out to Aston Hall, cos that's where old Lloyd lived, y'see. Well, as cocky as a fly on a bull's arse, he rides right up to the hall, through the gates and knocks on the door as if he'd been invited himself. As I said, he knocked on the door and when the servant comes to the door he says to give his greetings to Squire Lloyd, who as yer can expect was a mite surprised. Out comes Lloyd as red as a beetroot and he offers Wild 'Umphrey a drink y'see, all kind of polite. And of course 'Umphrey wasner one to turn down a free drink." The listeners chuckled.

"But while 'Umphrey was having his drink, Lloyd's men were shutting the gates and getting ready to nab him. But Wild 'Umphrey was having none of it. He drinks up, slips the silver mug in his pocket and as cocky as anything says 'Farewell, Squire Lloyd' and away he goes on his horse right over the gates and guards before they knew it.

They all laughed and uttered approving comments.

"Ar, he's a rum un. They canner catch him. He's too sharp for them."

"No, yer right there." Came back the chatty old man, "They couldner catch him because y'see, when they got themselves roused and after him, they all goes the wrong way, cos Old Nick, his horse, has his shoes on backwards, so old Lloydies men ends up back at Montfords bridge."

They all laughed again and had another drink.

Chapter Four

CROWDS FLOWED OVER the Welsh Bridge into the township of Shrewsbury, all come to the monthly wool and cloth market. It was a big occasion and much else, festivities, horse sales and so on were held on the periphery of the cloth sale. Thus people from miles around, both rich and poor would come.

Many people riding, on foot or by cart, were proceeding along the western route from Welshpool, Oswestry and further afield. Some were drapers with their carts laden with the recently purchased cloth from the Welsh market. There were gentle folk come more for the social occasion than for business; it was an opportunity to meet kinsman and other members of the gentry with whom they could discuss the politics of the day and the economic state of affairs. They rode usually but some came in carriages, especially if they were bringing with them their lady-folk. They were all dressed splendidly and ornately, standing out from and above the commoner people who swarmed around them, who also came mainly for the social side of the market. Amongst them were small time peddlers with trinkets or others selling vegetables or fruit, some carried grinding stones on their backs offering to sharpen knives and others were simply knaves come for some fun and enjoyment. All were ragged and unshaven though a conspicuous exception was the so-called friar on his mangy mule offering relics of all kinds from the finger of John the Baptist to a lock of hair from the Archbishop of Canterbury. He was a bigger villain than many of the ruffians who also trooped towards the market after rich pickings, pick-pockets and thieves of all sorts.

Amongst this crowd one could hardly notice two scruffy unshaven horsemen on mangy mud-splattered mounts. They slouched along on their mounts hardly speaking. They both looked tired and miserable. The one, on a scruffy old mare, had scraggy black hair falling in tangles over his shoulders and a rough-cut misshapen black beard and moustache covered the rest of his features. His garb, though not dirty, was scruffy and torn; he wore an ill-fitting waistcoat and a faded brown cloak. His companion looked no better, except that he only had a moustache and no beard, revealing a narrow prominent chin and thin, soft lips. They plodded on and took their place in the queue to cross the bridge. It was a narrow bridge at either end where stood two turrets, though it widened out a little in the middle. It would allow only one cart to cross at a time and it was this fact that was causing the obstruction and delay.

"Make way there, make way you ruffians!" Shouted a gentile voice from further back in the crowd, and a mounted man flashing his whip in all directions forced his way through the crowd followed by a finely finished covered carriage.

"Make way, I said. Have you no respect?" and the gentleman barged on whip in hand. He barged past the two ruffians on horseback bawling at them as he passed. The one made a move as if he would correct the gentleman's manners but the other made him stay his hand. The coach rattled past.

"Hold that damn cart. We shall cross first." Commanded the gentleman.

"Yes, sir." Responded the guard on the bridge and he pushed back the peddler trying to bring in his produce.

"Get out the way, you! Wait your turn!" The peasant tried to object but the guard slapped him down with various curses and threats. The coach passed and as it did, such was the proximity that all could see the inmates. One old gentleman, grey-haired, plump and covered in whiskers sat facing an equally plump and dignified old lady, beside whom sat rather meekly, or so it seemed from the outside, a young lady, who as far as any onlooker could judge in the semi-darkness of the coach, was of very fair complexion with long beautiful auburn tresses. The coach crossed.

The commotion caused by the very ungentlemanly gentleman having soon subsided, the procession of carters, peddlers and others continued. The two scruffy riders passed by the guards at either end of the bridge without any sign of recognition. Soon they were across.

"Well, we are in Tom." Said the less hairy fellow, when they were well out of earshot of the guard.

"Yes, Thank heaven. I cannot wait to have this thing shaved off and be cleaned up. I feel terrible." Said the hairier one called Tom, rubbing irritably at his growth. The other laughed,

"You look almost like Hopton." He joked.

"I should not mention that name too loudly while we are here." Responded Tom slightly reprovingly. The less hairy rider stroked his moustache musingly.

"I think I shall keep this. It rather becomes me, don't you think?" he said. The other only snorted and they rode on without another word along the cobble-stone streets. They passed the market place where already the drapers were displaying their wares and other peddlers were setting up their makeshift stalls. They trotted on only sparing it a glance. Soon they reached the head of the Wyle and passed by, on their right hand side, a large inn outside stood an expensive coach.

"Is that not the coach of that blaggard on the bridge? The one over there in front of the Lion?" asked the moustached rider with interest.

"Yes, it looks like it. It was good fortune that I was with you, otherwise you would have run him through."

"That's right." Laughed the other and still looking back at the carriage and the Lion Inn he began the descent of the Wyle, a short steep hill. His companion followed. The slowly descended the steep hill heading towards the river, which almost surrounded the town. But before they reached the bridge crossing the river to go back out of the town, the pair of horsemen turned into a courtyard through an archway, both belonging to the coaching inn alongside, 'The Unicorn' which was situated at the bottom of the Wyle.

They dismounted and declining the help of the stable-boy stabled and unsaddled their own horses. They walked across the yard to the inn, where they obtained some rooms, to which they immediately went.

An hour later two clean smartly dressed young gentlemen met at the bottom of the stairs. The one was completely clean shaven but the other, who could now be recognised as being the younger, retained a thin black moustache of the Spanish style.

"What do you think of it then, Thomas? Quite good, eh?"

"Very nice indeed" said Thomas cheerfully "You were right, Humphrey, it does suit you. I must admit you are very smartly dressed. For any particular purpose?"

"Personal business, my dear brother." Replied Humphrey eagerly, "I shall see you later." With this simple farewell he strode out, his black knee-length riding boots shining magnificently. Thomas watched smiling after him.

Humphrey Kynaston was as wild and impetuous as ever. Thomas did not need to strain his mind too much to guess where his young step-brother had gone.

Humphrey strode boldly back up the hill he had only an hour or so earlier descended. His stride was lively and bouncing and a boyish grin was on his lips and in his eyes. On reaching the top of the hill he turned into a bold entrance, nodding jauntily at the wooden lion over the door. Straightening his moustache he entered the inn. Without hesitation he sat down in a very plush, comfortable chair and ordered himself a glass of port, which although expensive, he could easily afford, even if he did prefer the ale in the Pigeons or the Wolf's Head. When the maid brought over the port he ordered himself a meal of pheasant, which he felt he richly deserved. When it arrived he ate heartily. By subtle conversation with the maid he easily learned the ownership of the splendid carriage, which he had seen earlier outside, for this as his brother had guessed, had been his mission. The carriage was the property of one Meredith ap Howell ap Morris of Oswestry, the old plump man whom Humphrey had seen through the carriage window. The plump old lady sitting opposite was obviously his wife and the young lady, presumably his daughter. And the young gentleman on horseback, as the maid secretively disclosed was the young lady's betrothed. The old man was both a rich merchant and a gentleman and thus this visit was for business and pleasure; for the old merchant, business, and for this wife and daughter, pleasure. All of which information greatly pleased Humphrey as did his dinner of pheasant. His mission accomplished and his appetite satiated he had another port and returned to his own, not quite so stately, temporary place of residence.

That evening Thomas returned with some urgent news.

"I have just spoken to Hopton and some others," he told Humphrey, "and they tell me your presence in Shrewsbury is already suspected by the Sheriff. He has ordered an increase in the town guard." Humphrey was silent. He led his brother to a quiet corner in the inn and sat down. Thomas continued,

"They suppose someone recognised you and reported it, but they are not sure."

"Ah, it is probably nothing. There are always rumours and tales. I have too much on my mind to bother with such hindrances." Humphrey simply shrugged it off. He rose to his feet and walked towards the stairs.

"I shall try to find out more" called Thomas, but his brother was not listening, he was already on his way to bed.

Next morning when Thomas rose he found that his impetuous young brother had already gone. Thomas was not too anxious, though a little suspicious. After a small breakfast he also left. He went to the dingy back streets of the town where the cheap, dirty taverns were, where normally he would have expected to be drinking and gambling if he had not something better to do. Amongst these taverns, where flourished pick-pockets, ruffians and thieves of all types and where he did not feel nearly as at home as usually did his brother, it did not take him long to find the man he was looking for.

"Five and Six" bellowed a booming voice, "I win. Ha, ha, ha!"

Thomas turned and followed the voice, an unmistakable voice to anyone who knew it. No-one could have a voice like that except Robert Hopton. Thomas followed the voice till in a dark corner at a dice table he recognised two white rims of eyes and a pair of huge, red lips shining from the wet of the ale. As he came closer the black mop and fuzz became partly visible.

"Robert, a word with you." Thomas beckoned him out of the corner. Like a bear coming from his den Hopton rose and followed.

"Av a drink, my friend Tom." He bellowed.

"No thank you," whispered Thomas, "It is a little early for me. Have you any more news?" Hopton looked blank.

"About Humphrey?" Thomas persisted. Sudden realization spread across what little of Hopton's face as could be seen, namely his nose and eyes.

"Oh, ar. Well," he began, lowering his voice, a thing of great difficulty and effort for him.

"We found out who gave the word to the sheriff. So last night me and some others got him. He won't tell no more stories, I can tell yer, ha, ha." He paused a little, "But we were too late. The story's all about the town now. Everyone knows he's here. He'll have to get out as soon as he can. I'll help if I can."

"Yes, I know that." returned Thomas, "But Humphrey does not yet want to leave. He has some woman on his mind."

"Ar, that's nothing new" guffawed Hopton.

"But there is something new about this one. She is of the gentry." Perhaps Hopton showed surprise at this but it was impossible to see.

"I shall attempt to persuade Humphrey to leave," continued Thomas, "But meantime, I shall stay in contact with you. Let me know if anything more occurs. Farewell." He left. Hopton returned noisily to his game of dice.

By the time Thomas had strolled back to the Unicorn, it was midday and lunch was being served. He was becoming more and more worried about his and Humphrey's predicament. If the Sheriff did have suspicions and did increase the guard, it would be very difficult to make an escape. What is more, in a town of this size, despite the increased population due to the market, it would not be difficult for the Sheriff to find the pair. Any villain, all of whom probably knew of Kynaston's whereabouts one way or another, would give the information for the right price. These thoughts had been troubling his mind as he strolled to the inn and now finding Humphrey finally he confronted him with them.

"Don't bother me about that," Humphrey complained, "I cannot leave yet. She is beautiful, you know, absolutely beautiful."

"Who?" interrupted Thomas. He knew who Humphrey meant but asked as he was annoyed with him.

"Isabella" answered Humphrey. He went on to explain to his uninterested step-brother how he had risen early and again gone to the 'Lion', how he had seen the father go off to business and how he had then, by chance, bumped into the mother and daughter, while they waited for their carriage. Enquiring whether they knew Shrewsbury well, he had to show them the sights and the old lady had been so charmed by such gallantry that she had accepted. The daughter, of course, had come along as well. He hastened to add that the daughter's betrothed had unfortunately been called to urgent business with his future father-in-law, whom he was directed by some anonymous messenger to meet in the market square, the merchant in fact being at the horse auction at the opposite end of the town.

Humphrey Kynaston could not stop talking about the outing and the beautiful girl he had accompanied. She had long, beautiful soft auburn hair, which fell lightly about her shoulders. Her eyes were always sparkling with life, happiness and understanding and her soft, sensitive lips shone out from her round, healthy face always in a radiant smile. Thomas eventually became so bored with the conversation, or monologue, that he simply stood up and went to his room.

That evening Humphrey was again smartly dressed and pruned as he strode once again from the Unicorn, turning right to ascend the Wyle. Thomas, looking from his room, saw him and guessed he had contrived to meet the merchant's daughter, whom he had called Isabella. Thomas wondered again if Humphrey's fancy might cost them both their freedom or even their lives.

Humphrey strode boldly and unconcernedly up the hill. He followed his previous footsteps which led him straight to the Lion Inn. He sat down in the plush armchair in the equally plush front room. Beautifully carved chairs and tables were in abundance, ornate oak panels festooned the walls and the fire-place was nothing less than a work of art, all of which Humphrey scarcely noticed. His mind, as could be expected, was elsewhere. In fact he was intent on over-hearing a conversation between two gentlemen in the corner of the room.

"Well, I am damned if I know who could have sent such a message" said the arrogant, pompous one. "Some damned scoundrel, I should think. I should give him a beating, were I to come across him." Kynaston chuckled to himself.

"Well, I certainly sent no message, my dear sir. Perhaps it was meant as a jest." Smiled the benevolent old gentleman, who was of course the Welsh merchant, the other being his future son-in-law, who simply snorted at the last comment.

"At least it did not spoil the ladies' morning. I hear from Isabella that they had a splendid time touring the town." Added the merchant, "Where are they now?"

"I left them in the parlour," said the betrothed with a slight note of contempt, "I became tired of their women's talk. Such idle chatter . . ."

Without waiting to hear any more of the conversation Humphrey rose from his table and calmly walked away. But he did not leave the inn; instead he went in the opposite direction. He went of course to the parlour, which, though not quite so splendid as the front room, was much more homely and comfortable especially as a small fire crackled away in the fire-place. But what made it so attractive to Humphrey was the company.

The ladies, on espying the young gentleman, who had shown them around Shrewsbury that morning, immediately called him over.

"Good evening, ladies." Humphrey saluted them, "By another fortunate coincidence we meet again." He looked into the smiling face of the younger lady, who seemed to be laughing knowingly behind the smile. Her dark-blue eyes flashed musingly into his own and in that moment they learned much about each other.

He joined the two ladies and spent the rest of the evening with them, talking of trivialities with the mother who was simply charmed by the young man. Humphrey put up with her idle and dull conversation, compensated by the stunning presence at her side. At every opportunity he tried to turn the conversation to Isabella, her life, her childhood, hopes and dreams but on nearly every occasion the mother would manage to turn the conversation back to some trivial, commonplace subject. But although the young couple exchanged only a few words, many glances were exchanged and many thoughts shared. When Isabella did speak, Humphrey could hardly keep his eyes from her soft lips, which formed the most beautiful shapes and curves while she spoke. She had a certain way of shaking her head when laughing so that her hair waved from side to side and a certain radiant smile which would accompany it.

The evening passed quickly for Humphrey despite the monotonous chatter that the mother managed to keep up, but for the two young people much had happened. Finally the two gentlemen returned suitably intoxicated to retire to their rooms. The broad shouldered, square headed one, betrothed to Isabella and whose name was Anthony Mytton, related as he boasted to the great local family of that name, scowled at the trio as he came in.

"Do you not think it time you retired, Isabella?" he said sternly, scowling again at Humphrey.

"My dear Anthony" she jibed, her eyes laughing, "I am not yet your wife to command in such a manner." Mytton was struck dumb."

"Yes, it is getting rather late. I think we should all retire" interposed the old gentleman diplomatically. The ladies rose and accompanied by the merchant left to retire to their rooms. Isabella openly held out her hand in farewell to Kynaston, who accepted and kissed it gently. Mytton remained behind.

"I hope you have no intentions on Isabella," he growled, "For your information we are betrothed and if you have any intentions I will personally make you suffer for them." He stared menacingly and arrogantly into Kynaston's face. Humphrey stood up.

"If I have any intentions on Isabella, as you put it, I certainly can not see what business it is of yours." Humphrey, not quite the height of Mytton, stared back from very close proximity into the hard, cold eyes of his opponent. They stood transfixed. The top of Mytton's lip twitched. Humphrey strode past him and walked out of the main doorway.

"Humphrey! Where on earth have you been? We must leave immediately."

Humphrey spun around to the voice from the dark.

"We must leave, Humphrey. We have no more time." He recognised it as the voice of his brother.

"Pardon" he said.

"We must leave" repeated Thomas, stepping from the darkness of the alleyway and tugging urgently at his younger brother's sleeve. Humphrey stood bemused, smiling into his face. He raised his eyebrows in amused enquiry.

"I have seen Hopton again and he tells me the Sheriff is hot on your trail. There is no time at all to lose." Thomas paused. Humphrey was silent. The meaning had been made apparent. Thomas continued a little less excitedly.

"Somebody gave information on your whereabouts and somebody from the Unicorn also recognised you. There are guards all around the inn at this very moment."

"What about you?" asked Humphrey, calmly but concerned. He was again thinking as a highwayman, "Have you been recognised?"

"No, I do not think so," replied Thomas, slightly bewildered.

"Well then, you may stay. Only I have to leave." He stood meditatively. "But first I must get my old mare. I have no chance without her. I have a plan though. Goodnight Thomas, sleep well!"

"What?" Thomas looked completely bewildered.

"Goodnight. Act as if nothing is wrong, simply return to your room. I shall handle everything else. Do not worry."

With that Humphrey turned sharply and retraced his steps back up the hill from the dark alleyway where Thomas had apprehended him. Thomas still stood bewildered and speechless at the reaction of his brother. Humphrey disappeared into the darkness.

A few minutes later a dark figure could be seen creeping around the back of the Lion Inn. It leaped cat-like, smoothly and silently, from the ground to the stable roofs. Softly it padded along the roof. Crouching down it sleuthed along the apex till it reached the main building, then again it leaped. It landed silently on the balcony. It tapped on the window quietly but hurriedly. Nothing. Again it tapped but still nothing. It tapped harder this time.

"Humphrey!"

Isabella stood in the window.

"Please have no fears, my dear Isabella." He touched her warm hand gently. "I must leave Shrewsbury immediately, but I am in dire need of your help." Humphrey looked into Isabella's keen eyes. They were soft, warm and inviting. Her hand shivered a little in Humphrey's.

"I must leave, but I will see you again." His lips quivered as he spoke. He began again but faltered. Though there was no moonlight, the rhythmic swelling of her breasts could plainly be seen, soft and white, only half enveloped by the nightdress. Her eyes were no longer laughing but in earnest. Humphrey opened his mouth once more to say something, but he did not speak. He leant forward and his lips met hers, so succulent and so delicate. She responded.

Chapter Five

Two guards stood leaning against the archway of the Unicorn Inn courtyard. A few more lay hidden in the darkness. The cold was beginning to reach their bones and they shuffled irritably. Their feet felt like the cobblestones beneath them. Hard and cold. Now and again their eyes would click shut despite the cold, but after only a few seconds sleep they would shake themselves back to their semi-wakefulness. For hours they had waited and more hours they expected to wait. They had set upon some occasional drunken ruffians but their efforts had gone unrewarded. Only a few minutes earlier footsteps had been heard but when challenged it was found to be an old hag who slept in the stables. They had laughed at her and perhaps thought to have some fun but she was too old and they were too tired anyway.

CRASH!

The stable doors flew open and a dark shadow on a dark steed burst out and rushed for the archway.

"The devil! It's the devil, run!" screamed a terrified guard and they all took his advice. The pair galloped up the hill and along the High street towards the bridge. They would have to cross it to escape. The mare's hooves were muffled as they rode over the cobbles, wrapped as they were in sacking.

"Halt in the name of the King!" commanded a guard as the dark figures suddenly came into view. Another guard rushed to his side. The muffled hooves persisted unchecked.

"Shut the gates!" called the one and the gates were duly shut. Humphrey slowed his mare seeing his escape barred.

"Halt and surrender yourself!" repeated the guard but Humphrey was in no mood for surrendering. He drew his sword and charged. The two guards leaped from the path of the lunging horse and the pair rode on unopposed straight towards the river. Humphrey dug in his spurs and urged the mare on. She neighed and reared. She would not jump. In the darkness the swirling torrent of the flooding river below was too much even for this brave mare.

The two guards collecting themselves, converged on the fugitive and from just off others could be heard running, attracted by the commotion. The guards grabbed at the mare and at Kynaston's legs. He slashed down with his sword and his mare slashing with her hooves dealt with the other, crunching his ribs. Again Kynaston dug in his spurs but his faithful companion still would not jump. The other guards could be heard coming nearer and nearer.

"Jump, old gal. Jump!" he yelled but she would not. Pushing her once more towards the bank, Kynaston leaped himself leaving his horse behind. The guards rushed up but they were too late. They stood looking into the black swirling void below them and shuddered. No-one could possibly survive. They turned back to their wounded comrades groaning on the ground.

By the next morning it had been reported to the Sheriff that the notorious outlaw, named 'Wild Humphrey' had met his demise in a vain attempt at escape by swimming the flood-swollen Severn. In not more than one hour the notices were being posted throughout the town to the same effect, thus the whole town was informed of this significant event, if they did not already know through the grapevine.

According to their position in society the population either raised a relieved toast or muttered some mournful obituary,

"Poor bugger, he wanner so bad. What a way to go."

In the upper echelons of society there was much relief and not a small amount of celebration. At most dinners or entertainments the highwayman's death was the main talking point for some time afterwards. Had Humphrey Kynaston still been alive he would have been proud and gratified that he should remain in the memory of so many people.

In fact he would not only be proud and gratified but also greatly amused. As indeed was the scruffy little sweep, who sat huddled up sipping a pint of ale in the dingy corner of the 'Plough'.

"Ar, that Wild 'Umphrey was a good 'un, sure enough" someone was saying, "He never done us folk any harm, I know."

"He gave the old Sheriff a run around afore they got 'im" chuckled another.

"But they never did catch 'im. He was a fly one alright."

The sweep, chuckling to himself, stood up revealing that he was taller than an onlooker might have at first expected and he sloped off through the narrow doorway. He limped to the stables where having disappeared for a few minutes he re-emerged leading a fine mare, too fine one would have thought for a dirty sweep like him. But, nevertheless he led the horse unremarked through the Shrewsbury streets and over the Welsh Bridge. Once over the river the sweep's physical defects miraculously seemed to right themselves and pulling off the old sacking covering the horse he swung nimbly up into the saddle and waving a defiant fist at the mystified guards Humphrey rode away.

Despite the reported death of Humphrey Kynaston the authorities were surprised to notice that the robberies still persisted. In fact it appeared that they increased in their frequency and daringness. Merchants, rejoicing that they could drive unmolested to Oswestry, were robbed in broad daylight by some robber-knight fitting the exact description of the presumed late Humphrey Kynaston. More and more rent-collectors were being ambushed and the Sheriff was simply bewildered.

On the other hand the locals at the Wolf's Head and the Three Pigeons were simply roaring their heads off and bellies out with laughter at the expense of the Sheriff. Humphrey had related to them how having swam across the river he had acquired some old sweeps clothes and simply returned to the town the next day to collect his mare, which he found grazing under the town walls. There had been no trouble at all, he said, in going in and out of town as the guards, presuming him dead, were so relaxed. Even had they recognised him, he joked, they would have been too frightened to move, presuming him to be a ghost.

The person most pleased at the resurrection was his brother, Thomas, who had been in such deep mourning at the reported death that he had, of all things, been considering giving up this unlawful way of life and even of surrendering himself to the Sheriff. Thomas was relieved that he was saved from making such a futile and disastrous step.

When the Sheriff finally realized what a fool he had been made to look and inundated by complaints from infuriated merchants and local gentry, he had no option but to increase the efforts to catch the notorious robber. Indeed he felt so humiliated that he swore he would not rest until the outlaw was swinging from a gibbet. Anyone who knew anything about Humphrey could have predicted that the Sheriff would have a long restless wait.

About a month after his escapade in Shrewsbury Humphrey learned that a certain rich merchant, accompanied by his wife and daughter, were due to return to Oswestry following a prolonged stay in the county town. Such an opportunity, thought Humphrey must in no way be wasted. He could combine two missions in one; he could perform another robbery as well as seeing once again the beautiful Isabella. Her vision engulfed his mind, her eyes, hair, lips, breasts. It all flooded back as he stood again at the mouth of his cave looking out. Ever since his escape over the river every spare moment had been used up in thinking about her. She was completely different from all his previous mistresses; he could not keep her out of his mind. His feelings were mixed as he continued staring, he was apparently watching but from the emptiness of his eyes it was obvious his mind was elsewhere. He longed to see Isabella again and this was an opportunity. He wondered if she would recognise him or would she be too shocked and horrified. But perhaps she would not be filled with revulsion. She might sympathise with him, overlook or perhaps even admire his reckless way of life. He did not know what to think. But this did not matter as it was not his thoughts that were governing his actions at this time, but his emotions. So distracted was Humphrey that he did not immediately notice a carriage appearing on the highway. He had let it almost pass by beneath him before he was shaken from his reverie.

Once spurred into life Humphrey took only a minute to scramble down from his cave and mount his horse. Once again they followed the path down the steep hill. When he reached the highway the carriage had already passed. He started in pursuit. The driver realising the threat struck out with whip and rein, despite which the highwayman had soon overtaken them.

"Hold your horses, or they shall drop where they stand." He raised his sword menacingly. The horse stopped. The old merchant looked from inside the carriage.

"What is the purpose of this, Sir? You indeed have a great nerve threatening my man in such a manner. Move from our path immediately or you shall have cause to regret your action."

Indeed these were strong words from the normally genial gentleman, whose rotund face now flushed brightly under the greying hair. Without reply Humphrey trotted closer, his sword naked in his hand.

"The devil!" exclaimed the old merchant, "You are the gentleman we met in the town of Shrewsbury over a month since."

"What? Why, yes it is" spoke the old lady looking out as well, "He was so charming. How lovely to see you again, young man!"

"The pleasure is all mine, I can assure you." replied Humphrey politely but ominously.

"Put away your sword young man, we have no quarrel with you. What business have you with us?" asked the stern, blustery face of the merchant.

"Ah, yes" began Humphrey, "I am indeed here on a matter of business. I have a proposition to put to you, master draper." Humphrey still held his sword threateningly.

"Well, come to it, sir, and put away your sword."

Ignoring the command of the merchant Humphrey continued,

"I suggest, sir, that I relieve you of your heavy purse in exchange for your continued safe conduct to Oswestry. I think you would agree that is a fair proposition."

"You blaggard! You shall have none of my money" retorted the old man defiantly. Another voice spoke from within the carriage amidst shocked exclamations from the merchant's lady wife,

"I knew you were a rogue the first I set eyes on you. You shall not get away with this."

"Ah, master Mytton, I presume" smirked the outlaw, "and how, may I venture to ask, do you intend to prevent me?" He came right up to the side of the carriage and held the point of his sword at Mytton's chest. The lady shrieked again.

"Do not fear, madam. I intend no harm to any person, if I receive what I came for." With this word Humphrey glanced into the corner of the carriage at the fair Isabella. Even in the shadow he could perceive her glinting eyes and pure white skin. He wondered what she now thought of him, now knowing his true profession. She sat silently, herself thoughtful and full of wonder. She could give no hint of her feelings, even if she understood them herself. She simply met his glance with an energetic, inquisitive, glinting flash of her lovely deep-blue eyes.

"If you were not at the advantage of a weapon, I should have you skinned alive" blurted Mytton, flushed and sweaty, still at the point of the outlaw's sword.

"Hand over your purse, merchant, or your brave companion might suffer!" said Humphrey calmly but threateningly.

"You would not dare!" retorted the draper, still defiant and furious. But nevertheless he handed over a number of purses, which needless to say, Humphrey accepted gratefully. Checking the contents quickly, he slipped them into his saddle pocket.

"Thank you kindly. I hope we may have many such business deals in the future."

The merchant muttered some oaths under his breath.

"We will meet again, blaggard," threatened Mytton, "and the next time I shall be prepared. You are obviously this Kynaston fellow that the whole county is talking about. Your death will be welcomed by us all."

"I thought I had heard that the fellow was dead. Drowned, so the tale goes." Humphrey laughed. He could afford to with his sword in hand.

"I shall also look forward to our next meeting" he sneered poking Mytton in the chest with his sword point, "and I look forward even more so to our next engagement, Isabella" he said, his voice softening as he nodded in her direction, "for indeed I intend to see you again."

She stared intensely up into his ravenous eyes. She seemed to beckon him, to dare him to take such a risk. She seemed to be taken as much as Humphrey with the prospect of the challenge. This Humphrey thought he recognised and hoped was true, but perhaps it was just his imagination.

"Farewell till then" Humphrey finished, sheaving his sword. He turned his horse and galloped back into the safety of the dense forest, leaving the inhabitants of the carriage wondering about this strange interlude. The old merchant defiant, furious, determined on revenge but helpless. The old lady making trivial exclamations about everything being so strange and how such a nice young man could do such a thing. She rambled on while Mytton silently seethed. Also silent sat Isabella; meditative, but she did not seethe for revenge. Her imagination had been fired by the daring and handsome outlaw, who had made both her father and her husband-to-be look inept fools.

Still furious and still absolutely helpless, the merchant leaned again through the window,

"Drive on, man!" he shouted at the driver and they continued on their way to Oswestry.

Once again at his cave Humphrey watched the carriage plod out of sight, crawling along the rough track at an almost painful pace. Painful to Humphrey for it was taking away the woman he so deeply desired.

In the following weeks Humphrey was plagued not only by the militia, which he accepted as an occupational hazard, but also by his thoughts. It took little guessing to know to where his thoughts were directed. Now when he stood upon his hill his eyes stared not straight out west over the land of his ancestors but, perhaps unconsciously or perhaps not, his eyes directed themselves more towards the north. Behind the glazed distant brown eyes thoughts were tumbling around. Perhaps his mind was filled with the sight of a carriage plodding its way along a dirty rough track, its size dwindling and dwindling till it is almost invisible, but never quite. It still lingers, miniscule in size, but it never disappears. It is still there even though it has gone, like the peal of bells, the thirteenth chime.

Perhaps a vision of sparkling eyes and shining lips engulfed this mind blocking out all other hint of thought. Eyes flashing out of a darkened carriage, the lips just visible as the light catches them for only a moment. But such a long moment, an infinity.

Perhaps his mind was more conscious. He may have been thinking of whether or not his infatuation was returned or even were it so what ever could become of such a relationship. An outlaw and a merchant's daughter. Was it possible? Was he too old? For age was beginning to leave its mark on Humphrey the Wild. His thick black hair was beginning to thin out and the toll of the elements and a rough and active life were to be shown on his face. He was now approaching forty and the question had to be faced, how much longer could he continue with his wild and riotous way of life. Perhaps the question also plagued his mind as to whether the young and fresh woman he desired might not consider him too old even if she could overlook or forgive the outlawry.

Anyone of these things would have been enough to have filled and blurred the outlaw's mind. Who could tell what thoughts lay hidden. Perhaps all these thoughts at once occupied him. But there again perhaps they didn't. Not even his horse would know and she was the only other one there.

In fact she did not care. She was quite happily pulling away at some hay at the base of the rock, as is the wont of most horses at that time of year. And she probably would have carried on contentedly munching away had not the highwayman come down the rock-steps, saddle over his shoulder. The mare looked up, hay still protruding from her mouth.

Humphrey whistled and the mare trotted to her master, breathing in his face as he caressed her ears. Silently he saddled the sturdy mare who stood still and patient. She was as well trained as had been all of Kynaston's horses. For it was a fact that, despite stories to the contrary, Kynaston had worn out a few horses already in the course of his hectic life. Legend would have it that the outlaw still rode the same dark mare, which he had rode that fateful day when Hopton came to warn him of his peril and he had left his old estranged father quivering on the doorstep of the family residence. Humphrey had ridden away that day and never returned not even to visit his mother, before she herself had died. They had met frequently elsewhere and kept in contact through Thomas, who now alone held the castle. Now it stood through negligence in a terrible state of repair, not a shadow of the fine estate it had been in the old father's time. He would have turned in his grave had not the heavy tombstone kept him in his place.

That was all past now and almost forgotten by the outlaw. Since then his beloved mare had passed away, as had another which followed. The local peasantry would have none of this; the horse was almost as renowned as the outlaw himself. Named 'Old Nick' by the local folk, despite it being a mare, she was endowed not only with an apparent longevity but also powers of flight. How else could she continually evade the pursuits of the Sheriff?

Whether she could fly or not Kynaston flung the saddle over the horse's back and was quickly mounted. Soon the pair were tripping through the surrounding woodlands.

They appeared in no hurry as they leisurely made their way through the narrow tracks making sure to keep a good cover of thicket between themselves and the main road onto which they were loath to stray. They may have rode leisurely but still never complacent, both horse and rider were as alert as ever. Despite his mind being over-occupied with many varying thoughts and perhaps his mind being filled with visions other than the surrounding greenery, caution had become so much a way of life that it had become second nature.

Particularly of late Humphrey had to be extra cautious and hardly ever used the main highways. This was partly due to the robbery of the Oswestry merchant, for the frustrated little man was determined on revenge and had used all his influence to persuade the Sheriff to step up patrols along this route. If the merchant was determined on revenge there were no words to describe the feelings of the humiliated Mytton, who had added the weight of his family name in the effort to increase the forces and activities of the militia. Mytton himself had offered to recruit and lead a small force in an all-out attempt to apprehend the outlaw, perhaps with a direct attack on the cave or the taverns of the cut-throats and thieves. So far the cautionary words of the Sheriff, as to the possibilities of success of such a dangerous action, had prevailed. But Mytton continued to seethe.

Nevertheless the patrols along the Oswestry to Shrewsbury road had been increased despite the paucity of men available. Many of those recruited would have preferred to remain at home rather than risk danger. They were not soldiers or swordsmen. Most joined, or were conscripted, for the lack of any other employment and in some cases the term able-bodied would have been more than a little of an over-statement. Even so Humphrey thought it wiser in the present circumstances not to chance a confrontation.

He trotted on along the back woodland tracks emerging eventually at the head of a small rise, at the bottom of which, invitingly, stood the Wolfs Head inn. Nothing seemed amiss so he rode to the side of the inn and tied up his dark mare.

He stepped into the darkness of the inn through the side door. A mixture of ale, sweat and dankness rose to his nostrils and by it's unfamiliarity it mildly disgusted him. He could not see perfectly at first for his eyes had not yet adjusted to the light, or better the lack of it. But he was immediately recognised.

"Ah, well, look who it be!" said one.

"It must be a ghost, I know" guffawed another and the whole inn erupted with laughter. But Humphrey took no notice. He was not in the mood. He had not been here for a while, neither had he been seen in his other favourite haunts. Rather out of character he had been keeping to his own company for most of the time, pre-occupied as he was with his distracting thoughts. By the time he reached the bar a jug of ale was already waiting for him, frothy and pungent. He grasped it and downed it all in one great gulp, beer and froth spilling down his cheeks. There was a great cheer from the assembled regulars, and he banged it down with a great show of achievement.

"Fill it up again, Landlord, and the same for everyone else in here!" Humphrey tossed a gold coin onto the bar and the landlord gratefully obliged. Another cheer erupted from the inhabitants of the bar and they began to rush up to refill their tankards. Soon they were all back at the gambling and raucous banter. Humphrey reluctantly joined in the fray. For a while at least the ale and the conversation would provide a distraction from his other preoccupations.

Chapter Six

The next morning he slowly woke from his drunken sleep. He looked around him. At first everything seemed unfamiliar. This wasn't his cave. There wasn't that smell of warm straw and sacking. He rubbed his eyes and made out the first rays of light coming through a small window and they gave just enough light to illuminate the small dark room with its bed and a few items of furniture. Clothes lay over the chair in the corner of the room, but they were not his. His eyes focused, gradually adjusting to the half light from the deep alcoholic sleep. They were clearly women's clothes. After a second or two to allow this information to penetrate his mind, he turned to look beside him to see his bed partner for last night. She was lying face down in the bed clothes so he could not immediately recognise her, but he guessed that it could only be one of the two serving girls from the inn below. He had by now realised where he was; lying in bed in the room over the Wolf's Head, where he had obviously spent the night. He couldn't remember too much about it. After his dramatic entrance things had settled down and everyone gone back to their past-times. He had probably played cards, obviously drank some more and laughed and flirted as he usually did, but he could not remember precisely. Anyway he had clearly ended up in bed with Nancy, whom he now recognised, even from her back, and spent the night at the inn. She rolled over as he sat there gathering his thoughts. Yes, it was Nancy. He congratulated himself on his ability to recognise her from behind. She gave a sleepy moan as she opened her eyes.

"Oh, hello darlin', are you alright?"

"Yes, I'm fine. You go back to sleep." Humphrey leaned down and kissed her on her cheek. She smiled briefly and then gratefully closed her eyes again. Humphrey climbed out of bed and fumbled around in the semi-darkness for his clothes. He splashed himself with some water from the jug and dressed quickly. Nancy woke again and raised herself up from the bed to look over.

"Oh, Humphrey, come back to bed. Come and keep me warm."

He walked over to the bed and leaned over once again and kissed her.

"No, I have to be away. I will see you another time." He kissed her again and began to leave. He grabbed his coat and reaching into his pocket he pulled out a gold coin and threw it onto the bed.

"Oh, thanks Humphrey" drawled Nancy. He pulled on his boots, wrapped his coat around him and with a wave and blowing another kiss he quietly slipped out of the room. He fumbled his way down the dark wooden stairs. Despite the gloom he found his way, for he had been this way many times before. At the bottom of the stairs he pushed open the old wooden door, which creaked on its hinges as it swung open, and he found himself once again in the main room of the inn. The smell of stale beer again greeted him. One or two bodies lay around over the tables, fallen asleep as they lay in a drunken stupor. As he walked between the tables the landlord stirred from the back room.

"Humphrey, you're up early! You're a bit early for breakfast, but I'll roust those wenches up and they can get you something in a little while."

"No, don't bother them. I do not have any appetite. I will get something later. I want to be on my way, I have a few hours ride ahead of me" replied Humphrey.

"Oh, on a mission?" quizzed the landlord, "Another profitable one, I hope"

"That's my business." came Humphrey's curt reply. "I will probably be back in a few days."

With that he strode out into the bright light of the new day. He shivered a little in the frosty air of the early morning. The sky was clear and the sun starting to rise. It looked like it was going to be a clear, sunny day. He felt good as he breathed in the cold, fresh air and strode towards the stable, where he could hear the faint rustling and noises of the horses. He pushed open the heavy double doors of the stable and enjoyed for a moment the pleasant odour of warm straw and the smell of horse. His mare whinnied as she recognised her master.

"Morning, my love. I hope you slept well, for we have a long ride ahead of us today." He walked over and stroked her neck as she leaned towards him.

"That's my girl. Let's get you saddled up then, shall we?"

He collected the saddle from where it was hanging and efficiently saddled his horse. Ten minutes later he was leading her out of the stables. Her hooves rattled on the stone yard as she was led across. Humphrey swung up into the saddle. He waved at the landlord, who now stood in the doorway of the inn, and trotted away.

The horse began to make its way on its usual route through the woods and up the steep hill but as she reached a fork in the track the rider turned her away.

"This way, my girl. Today we will set out on a different road."

The pair turned to the left hand track, which led more on the level and heading north-west. They trotted on at a steady pace, unhurried but clearly on a mission. They made their way towards the main road heading north-west towards Oswestry and onwards to Wales. The road was the busy road that he was well used to watching, keeping an eye out for merchants and coaches. But this time he was travelling it himself. It was the most direct route to where he wanted to go, but he knew that he would have to be very careful not to be recognised. The route was now patrolled on a fairly regular basis by the local militia and Humphrey knew that one of the people they were on the look out for was him. He would have to spot them before they spotted him. Luckily he knew all the side roads and back roads in order to avoid detection. On a number of occasions he spotted a small patrol up ahead and he simply turned off and disappeared into the surrounding greenery. Due to this necessary caution progress was relatively slow. But the pair persevered on their mission. By nightfall he had reached the outskirts of Oswestry and he became even more cautious. He made his way to one of the many inns of the town, where he proceeded to secure a room for the night. He took time to settle his mare down in the stables before going to his own quarters. Later he partook of a supper of beef stew and ale which he had sent up to his room. He did not feel like sharing company, which was unusual for the normally gregarious Humphrey. Compared to the night before he had a quiet evening and retired early to his bed.

He rose early in the morning, again declining breakfast. After settling up with the landlord he went over to the stable and saddled up his mare. She was pleased to see him again and she nuzzled into him as he fitted the reins. Soon he was on his way again and was relieved once he had passed by the town gates without any incident. The guards were hardly awake themselves and did not give the anonymous horseman a second glance. Humphrey trotted past them and away up the hill. Only when he had travelled a few hundred yards did he feel safe enough to stop and look behind. He pulled off the hood which had largely kept his face hidden. Oswestry was now behind him and the patrols would be no more. This was beyond his normal hunting grounds and was generally thought to be safe from highwaymen and other scoundrels.

But he was not here to extend his domain or to look for pastures new for his skulduggery. He had a different mission and he was not to be distracted from his purpose.

After another two hours steady riding he turned from the main road and headed higher into the Welsh hills passing fields of sheep, the main currency in the area. They were the source of his own wealth and means. For if it were not for the sheep there would be no wool market and no rich merchants. He was amused at the idea as he rode by the flocks in the fields and on the surrounding hills. The occasional shepherd looked across the fields as the dark rider passed by. They did not see too many riders coming this way and were naturally curious. The dogs temporarily distracted from their work barked, but the mare ignored them and trotted on by.

As he came over the brow of small hill he spotted a hamlet of a dozen homes and outhouses, smoke wisping its way from one or two. A few women were out going about their daily chores. Chickens and dogs wandered freely round. He approached the hamlet and the women looked up at the lone rider and ceased their conversations. Humphrey rode between the low wooden houses, the chickens dispersed and the dogs came to see who the stranger was.

Humphrey rode up to the small gathering of womenfolk, who were eying him up and down. A few small children also emerged from the hovels to see the stranger.

"Good day, ladies." He greeted them, "I think you would agree it is a lovely day, is it not?"

"It is sir," One woman replied "What brings you to these parts? I don't think we have seen you around here before."

"I have business with Meredith ap Howell ap Morris, the merchant. His estate must be nearby, I think. Perhaps you could direct me, good lady."

The woman blushed a little, being unused to being addressed as a lady. Humphrey often found that flattery got him a long way and this was to be no exception.

"Oh, yes sir. His estate is just about another two miles away. You should take the left fork of the lane up ahead and that will lead you towards the manor. You will cross a small river and soon after that you will reach the main gate. You can see the main house from there."

"That is most helpful. I shall bid you good day and please accept this as an acknowledgement of your help." Humphrey reached into his purse and handed her some coins.

Her eyes lit up at the sight and she gratefully accepted them. The others looked on surprised and envious. Humphrey touched his hat in salute and bade them farewell. He roused his horse and they trotted off on their way. As they reached the fork in the road ahead, he steered his mount to the left as directed and he disappeared from the view of the watching women and children. Life returned to normal in the quiet hamlet.

As directed the road led on over a brow and down a slope towards a small river. A solid rustic wooden bridge allowed for easy crossing. It was not at all ornate but had clearly been designed to allow for the safe passage of carriages and carts. The road itself was basic but again wide enough for carriages. The horse's hooves pounded on the thick wooden beams as they crossed and soon after they came to the large gates, which announced the entrance to the merchant's manor. The tracks of the carriages could easily be seen in the muddy track as they turned through the gates and upwards towards the fine manor house nestling between the trees at the end of the long drive. Beyond the gates the road narrowed and became less well looked after. It was muddier and more overgrown. It was this route that Humphrey decided to take, leading him temporarily away from his announced destination. He could see that it continued to lead uphill and so he followed for another half a mile, where from behind a large oak tree he could see clearly across the field to the back of the manor house. Here he would wait and watch.

He watched the various comings and goings of the servants at the back of the house, fetching water from the well and wood from the out house. Men were working in the fields some distance away. Others were in the stable yard cleaning out the horses and cleaning up the carriage that could be seen at the entrance to one of the farm buildings. Quite a hive of activity, mused Humphrey. He pulled some bread and cheese from his saddle-bag as he made himself comfortable on a small grassy knoll at the foot of the oak. He let his mare wonder around grazing along the hedgerows. He appeared to be in no hurry as he relaxed in the bright late winter sunlight.

As the sunlight dimmed and the darkness began to descend, the activity around the house appeared to diminish. Stable hands packed up and went off to their own quarters for supper. Other servants were busy in the kitchens preparing dinner for the merchant and his family.

Kynaston stirred himself. He patted his faithful mare, "You stay here my love. I will be back a little later. You have plenty to eat, so just stay nice and quiet till I return."

She nuzzled into him as if she understood his words.

Kynaston deftly climbed over a fence and through a hedge into the field beyond. He made sure to follow the hedge-line as far as possible as he made his way towards the manor house. In the gloom of semi-darkness he may still be picked out as an intruder in the open, but not up against the hedgerow. He easily made his way to the edge of the farm yard. Various outbuildings made it easy for him to remain out of sight of the main house as he crept ever closer to it. Some lights had now been lit inside the house. Down in the kitchen a lamp shone for the cook and kitchen maids. A lamp shone from the main dining room, where the table was being laid in readiness for the sumptuous meal in a few hours time. Kynaston crept around the building taking in all the activities. A few of the upstairs rooms also held a lamp, given away by the chink of light escaping through the curtains. Kynaston studied each room in turn. One of them had to be that of Isabella, probably preparing herself for dinner. He imagined her beautifying herself at her dressing table, brushing her hair and choosing which dress would be most suitable to wear. Perhaps she was being attended by her maid, helping with her hair and clothing. Kynaston mused on this.

He quietly slipped across the remainder of the yard unnoticed and leaned up closely by the wall of the manor house. He slid along the wall brushing past the shrubs and surrounding foliage. He skirted around to the back of the building where he could see some light on in the top windows. He scrambled up in a corner onto a low outhouse extension, near the kitchen. Carefully and as quietly as he could he crept across the low roof. Pulling himself to a narrow ledge he began to edge his way towards the bedroom windows he had seen from the ground. It was complete darkness by now and neither could he be seen or could he properly see where he was going.

He carefully edged his way around the corner of the building and reached the first of the bedrooms. He put his ear to the window and listened intently. At first he could hear nothing but gradually his hearing adjusted and he began to pick up on voices inside. After a few minutes he stealthily crept past the curtained window. He had recognised the voice of the older lady from the Lion Hotel, presumably Isabella's mother. He moved on to the next window. To his good fortune the window was slightly open in order to allow some fresh air. He could listen with ease.

He heard a female voice but he did not recognise it as that of Isabella. But shortly came a reply which he did recognise. His heart began to beat more quickly. It was Isabella, but her maid was also in the room. He would have to wait for an opportunity. Perched on the narrow ledge, in the darkness and with ever increasing cold, it seemed like an age to Kynaston as he waited. But he had to be patient. Eventually he heard the maid give her farewell and leave the room. Now was the time.

Kynaston tapped on the window. No response, so he tapped a little harder and more intently. He heard the rustle of a dress from inside as Isabella appeared to move nearer to the window.

"It is me. Your lover in the night." He whispered.

He heard a gasp from inside. This was the moment of truth. Would she call for help and give him away or did that night at the Lion Hotel mean something more to her? Humphrey held his breath and then whispered again,

"From the Lion Hotel. Surely you remember me."

He could hardly bear the silence, the uncertainty. Another rustle of clothing and a secretive movement of the curtains added to his apprehension. Isabella peeped through the chink in the curtains. She gasped again as she caught sight of the shadowy figure perched precariously of the ledge outside her bedroom window. For a long moment again there was silence.

"Come in" a hushed voice whispered. "I must turn down the lamp."

She disappeared back beyond the thick dark curtain. Humphrey opened the window slowly and stealthily climbed in. He pushed past the curtain and entered the softly lit bedroom.

Isabella turned around from lowering the lamp and gazed in amazement at the mysterious figure, which had emerged from behind the curtain. Confidently he now strode forward and held her in his arms. She threw her arms around him as he leant down to kiss her.

An hour later Isabella emerged from her bedroom and descended the stairs to the dining room. Neither her father nor mother noticed any great difference in her demeanour. They were already waiting and were in conversation as she entered the room. They had their own concerns and paid no undue attention to Isabella. She took her seat and the father gave instruction for the servants to begin to serve the meal.

"You are a little late, dear" noticed her mother finally during a pause in her conversation, "And you do look a little flushed. Are you well?"

"I am very well, thank you Mother. Perhaps I am just a little tired. I think I will retire early to bed straight after dinner."

"Probably a good idea. You do not want to become over-tired. You may catch a chill and that would not do. Yes, yes, you should retire early."

The mother then returned to conversation with her husband, who was bemoaning the down-turn in business and blaming it on that damned highwayman, putting off the traders and merchants. Isabella ate lightly and only partook in the conversation when directly questioned. Otherwise she was more than content with her own thoughts and feelings.

Above in the bed chamber Humphrey lay waiting. His hopes, his dreams and aspirations had all been fulfilled. He had been preoccupied with thoughts of Isabella ever since meeting her at the Lion Hotel that night. He lay on the bed looking up at the ceiling, drinking in the moment and drinking in the feeling of ultimate success. He stirred as he heard creaking on the floorboards outside the door and the door slowly began to open. He was ready to jump out and hide or run, but he was reassured by the soft tones of Isabella's voice,

"It is only I, Isabella, do not fear." She stepped quietly into the room looking around and was herself reassured to see Humphrey still waiting for her.

"I slipped away as soon as I could." She closed the door quietly behind her, checking that no-one was about outside. She walked towards the bed, stopping to slip off her dress and then slipped in beside Humphrey, who welcomed her with embracing arms. They kissed and once more fell into love making.

The cockerel crowed and Humphrey woke with a start. "Where was he?"

He remembered and he turned to see Isabella still sleeping beside him, her brown hair falling across her shoulder revealing the pale, soft skin beneath. He drank it in for a moment. The cockerel crowed again. Humphrey looked up as a shaft of light came in through the window and he realised with a start that he had slept too long. He had intended to slip away during the darkness of the early hours, but the sun was already of its way up and there was already some activity in the farm yard and kitchen. As he climbed out of the bed, Isabella stirred.

"What is it, my love." She sleepily asked.

"I must be away, my dear Isabella. I have over-slept and already there are workmen about in the yard. I must get away quickly. I am sorry but I must go now."

The urgency was reinforced as the chambermaid knocked on the door and was about to enter.

"No, not yet! Do not enter!" Called Isabella urgently, "Give me a moment to prepare myself. I will call for you shortly."

The maid thinking this unusual nevertheless respected her mistress's request and backed out of the doorway pulling the door as she did so. To herself in the corridor the maid pulled a quizzical face. But why should she worry, she could have a few minutes to herself. She shrugged her shoulders and walked off.

"I really do have to go, dearest Isabella, but never fear I will see you again as soon as I can."

Isabella checked the door and that the maid had properly gone. She then rushed up to Humphrey throwing her arms around him.

"Oh, please make it soon. I will die waiting." She gushed.

"I will do my best to get a message to you." They kissed. Humphrey hurriedly threw on his clothes and crept over to the window. Looking through the shutters he could see workmen moving around the yard outside, walking across to the stables. Two women walked around the corner of the building. Humphrey imagined they were heading towards the kitchen to start their work for the day.

For a brief moment the yard was clear. With his cloak over his head he opened the shutters and climbed out once again onto the ledge. He turned briefly to blow a kiss to

Isabella, who watched intently and anxiously. He felt his way along the ledge and when he reached the corner he peeped around. The maids had gone inside and he could hear light-hearted chatter coming from within.

In an instant he had slid onto the low roof and jumped to the ground. Staying flat against the wall for a second he glanced around and seeing the yard to be clear, he boldly walked across the yard as if he had all the right to be there. No-one noticed or took any heed of the man in the cloak as he marched past the stable door. If the stable hands did notice they took no real notice, imagining him to be a friend of the merchant on legitimate business. Either way it was not their business. A couple of dogs scavenging at the back of the kitchen looked up, but again were not disturbed by the stranger and soon went back to their more important task.

Soon the stranger had disappeared from view of the house and outbuildings and Humphrey could relax a little. He headed back to the fields he had crossed the previous night again keeping close to the hedge-line until he had finally reached the tree where his mare neighed in welcome.

"Oh, my love, have you missed me. Lets get you sorted out and we can be on our way and get some breakfast on our travels." The mare nuzzled him affectionately. As quickly as he could the highwayman untethered his mare, swung himself up into the saddle and quietly urged her to trot on back up the lane. Hidden by the thick hedgerows they were quickly out of sight of the manor and the surrounding fields. If any workmen spotted them, again they would think nothing

The Highwayman's Cave

of a well dressed stranger who had been visiting the rich merchant.

He soon reached the village where he had asked directions. Women were out and about doing their chores, men were setting up in their trades, the chickens scattered as chickens do and the dogs barked. This time the rider rode on by watched curiously by some of the women and children. He rode past back up the road, out of sight and out of mind.

About an hour's ride away on the road back to Oswestry Humphrey stopped at an inn. He dismounted and led his horse to the stables. A stable boy stepped forward.

"Look after my mare well, young man. Make sure she is warm and well fed and I will reward you well."

"Yes, sir" replied the lad eagerly. He led the mare away to be unsaddled, rubbed down, fed and watered. Assured, Humphrey took himself away to the inn to be fed and watered. He ordered himself a hearty breakfast and ale and sat himself down in a corner of the room.

It arrived in a short time and he heartily tucked in, ravenous after his nights adventures and exertions. He ate and drank up and ordered more ale to wash it all down. As he sat back at last satiated, the door opened and in walked two members of the local militia. Humphrey sank back into the corner where he sat, trying to blend in with the wall behind him. The men walked directly past him but paid him no particular attention. They called over to the inn-keeper, who was clearly familiar to them and ordered themselves some breakfast. They sat down on the opposite wall to him and immediately fell into conversation between themselves. Humphrey relaxed a little. He was not well known this far from his own usual haunts, but he always had to be alert. Although he was still an outlaw with a price on his head, not many people really knew what he looked like, beyond being tall and dark-haired, dressed in dark clothes and a dark cloak. But that description could apply to many a passing merchant or other stranger. The two militia men certainly did not seem to be on the look out for a highwayman in their midst.

Their food soon arrived and they greedily dived in. As they ate Humphrey heard them talk of a local landowner collecting his taxes. He could not help his ears straining to hear every detail. After all this was his chosen profession. They spoke of themselves meeting up with the tax collector, once his work was done and giving him a safe escort to the manor house. They joked about the threat of the highwayman.

"But he never comes this far. He's never been known up this way." The one claimed confidently.

"No, this'll be an easy job for us and good pay." The other agreed.

Finishing up his ale the stranger strode up to the counter to pay his bill.

"How much will that be for that wonderful breakfast?" He enquired of the inn-keeper, but before he received an answer he tossed some coins on to the counter,

"I hope that will cover it, my good host."

The man nodded in appreciation, "Oh, yes sir that will do very well. I am pleased that you enjoyed it."

Humphrey turned and walked confidently past the two militia men, he nodded politely at them as he passed but they barely responded, still engrossed in their own meal. He marched over to the stable and called the stable boy to saddle up his horse and bring her to him. She had been rested and fed, like himself and was ready and eager to be on the road again. Humphrey pressed a coin into the hand of the stable boy.

"Thank you very much sir." He was very pleased with his reward.

"You have looked after her well and you have earned it." He then swung up onto the saddle and with a parting wave to the stable boy, he rode off with his next venture clear in his head.

CHAPTER SEVEN

THE OPPORTUNITY OF ambushing a rent collector seemed too good to miss. The information that he had inadvertently overheard from the two loose-tongued militia men would prove very useful and hopefully very lucrative. Humphrey headed his mare off towards the area the men had spoken about, where the rent collector would be visiting the local villages and farms to extol the rent. Rent collectors were clearly never popular and it was this sort of ambush which had built up the highwayman's good reputation amongst the common people. He could afford to be generous and open with his money, when he acquired it so easily.

He trotted into one village and enquired as to whether the rent collector had visited or was due. He was told that the rent collector had visited them the previous week but today he was due in another hamlet about a further 8 miles away. Humphrey thanked the villagers for the information and dropped a few coins down to them, for which they were most grateful.

He rode on calculating that it would take about an hour to reach the next village, during which time he could contemplate his plan. As long as the collector was not protected by any soldiers or militia, Humphrey imagined that the process would be very straightforward. Once he had drawn his sword he was rarely confronted by a single rider and even if he was challenged, Humphrey was a very accomplished swordsman. Like most of his social class he had been raised to use the sword and lance, which skills may be called upon at times of war. As a gentleman he would be expected to respond at times of war, leading the local young men into action. Humphrey had enjoyed the practice of such weaponry and indeed had excelled at everything he had tried his hand.

At the time he had not imagined that he would be using such skills in the pursuit of highway robbery. He had dreamed of more honourable adventures fighting for his King and country.

When it came to the point of battle there were not many, if any, local militia men or bodyguards who had either the stomach or the ability to stand up to him. Faced with the highwayman most would think more of their own lives than the purse they were carrying or protecting. After a short verbal or sometimes physical exchange the purse would be dropped and the victim would be allowed to escape relatively unharmed. Humphrey would quickly collect his prize and gallop off in the opposite direction and soon lose himself in woods or hills, with which he was very well acquainted. It was only on a rare occasion that real blood letting took place, but clearly the incident leading to the death of 'the said John Hughes of Stretton' was one of these for which he had been outlawed.

Humphrey mused on that incident and the consequences it had brought with it. What would have become of him had that never taken place. He laughed to himself, for he knew well enough that if it had not been that incident that led to his outlawry, then another incident would have been along soon enough for sure. He knew himself well enough not to fool himself that things would have turned out differently. He had been young and reckless and this was the path it had taken him.

He quickly shook himself free of these thoughts and the fleeting regrets that they may have brought with them. He was now nearing the village where the rent collector was going about his business. He slowed his mount and warily went ahead. As he approached the village he became aware of a small gathering of men near the village inn. They were lining up outside to go in one by one to pay their rents to the collector, who had set up his stall in the inn. As one came out, another entered. Humphrey rode slowly past gesturing a greeting to the villagers as he passed. He dismounted and tethered his horse to a post. He sat down on the opposite side of the road, pulling out some bread and cheese, for again his appetite had been stimulated by the ride. He fed his mare some bread, which she eagerly ate. He acknowledged villagers as they passed and offered some greeting, but no-one thought it unusual for strangers to stop for a while to take a rest or some food and drink. The road was one of the main trading routes to Oswestry and many merchants and traders would pass through while going about their business. The line of men proceeded slowly, paying their yearly rent to the local landowner from whom they rented their farms. About lunchtime the procession had finished and after the rent collector had packed away his books, the inn returned to its normal business of refreshing the local population. At this point Humphrey himself decided to walk across to avail himself of the wares offered by the hostelry. He ordered a drink of ale and sat down in the darkened room. He could see across to the rent collector, who was being well serviced by the inn keeper with the best of food and drink on offer at the establishment. The collector was a valuable and revered customer. Humphrey took a good note of his face and identity. He would make sure to recognise him later out on the open road. He had not noticed any horse tethered outside, but imagined that the rent collector must have tethered it at the stable around the back of the inn. Again the collector's horse would receive the best of treatment.

Satisfied Humphrey stood up and carrying his cloak he strode past the rent collector as he went out. He walked down the road to the where his mare was tethered. He swung himself up into the saddle and trotted gently out of town, only attracting the occasional glance from one or two of the villagers.

The rent collector was due to move on to the next village for the afternoon to continue his work there. As Humphrey had overheard from the militia men, they were not due to meet him until after that and escort him back to the manor house. This left the rent collector unprotected until he reached the next village and this was clearly the opportunity that Humphrey intended to seize. He rode on out of sight of the village for about ten minutes and about halfway on to the next village. He picked out a small dense patch of woodland on a piece of raised ground. From here he could easily hide up and keep watch over the road and wait for the rent collector to appear. He casually gazed around the landscape but at the same time was thoroughly planning his escape route. He could see various patches of woodland through which he could make off and easily disappear from sight. He would then make his way back towards his own familiar countryside and the relative safety of his cave.

He had waited for almost half and hour before any one came into sight. Over the horizon a figure appeared on horse-back slowly walking along the track. As he came closer Humphrey recognised him as the rent collector. He had been well fed and watered at the inn and was in no particular hurry to reach his next appointment. In fact he was feeling positively drowsy having partook a little too much of the landlords generosity. As his mount reached the small rise the collector turned off the track and began to head straight for the wood in which Humphrey was hiding.

"What was he doing?" wondered Humphrey. He watched patiently but at the ready.

The collector trotted his horse up to the edge of the wood, where he dismounted and led the horse a little through the trees. Humphrey could no longer see well, so leaving his own horse tethered he crept slowly and quietly through the trees towards where the collector had entered the wood. As he crept closer he could hear the rustling of the horse amongst the undergrowth. He made sure he kept amongst the trees and circled around trying to get a better look. The collector had led his horse to a small clearing with a grassy bank. Humphrey could hear a snorting sort of sound, which he imagined to be the horse, but as he crept closer still he began to recognise it as the sound of someone snoring!

Humphrey could hardly believe his eyes or his good fortune. On the grassy bank lay the rent collector covered over with his coat stretched out fast asleep. Humphrey laughed to himself. So this was how the collector spent his afternoons. Well watered from the inn he intended to sleep off the ale before moving on to the next village, where he would be well fed and watered again. Imagining himself to be out of sight of any passers-by the collector was in the habit of taking a well-earned afternoon nap.

"How easy was this going to be!" mused Humphrey.

He waited and watched for five minutes or so to make sure that the collector was well away in the land of sleep. He was snoring well and deeply. Humphrey crept closer his sword in hand. The horse tethered at the edge of the clearing snorted as it spotted Humphrey coming through the undergrowth. Humphrey whispered quietly and soothed the horse. Gently he untethered the reins and led the horse away as quietly as possible, leading it to the edge of the wood he let it loose in the adjoining fields, where the horse gratefully trotted off to make the most of the abundant grazing.

In no time at all Humphrey was back at the clearing. The collector still lay snoring happily in the afternoon sun. He had the saddle-bag containing the rents as his pillow. Humphrey crawled on hands and knees as he quietly approached the snoring collector. He could easily slit the man's throat as he lay sleeping or he could just wake him with the sword tickling his throat. It was so easy. Too easy, perhaps. Humphrey rolled up his own cloak and reaching close up to the collector he laid the cloak next to the saddle-bag. Finding a woodpigeon feather nearby he reached over and gently tickled the ear of the collector. The collector tried to brush away the imagined fly but stayed asleep due to the amount of ale he had been proffered. Humphrey tried the feather again. The collector flicked again. Once more Humphrey tickled with the feather. This time the collector turned away from the annoying tickle and finding the soft cloak as a pillow his head gratefully sank into its folds. The tickling stopped and the collector sank into an even deeper sleep. Humphrey eased the saddle-bag away from the collectors head, sliding it silently along the smooth grass. He tiptoed away, disappearing into the woodland, leaving only the woodpigeon feather at the scene. He may have left his cloak but he felt that a good barter for the saddle-bag.

He had soon made his way back to his loyal mare waiting patiently for him, where he had left her at the other side of the wood. Quickly he threw the saddle-bag over across her shoulders and climbed up himself. Gently he encouraged her to move off across country down from the rise and away through the surrounding fields and woodlands. He glanced back and could see the collector's horse still happily grazing a little way from the woodland.

Chapter Eight

The roar of laughter rocked the rafters of the 'Wolf's Head'. The stories of the band of Welsh robbers who had stolen the rent collections had spread this far. Humphrey could only imagine the shock and wonder on the face of the rent collector as he awoke, finding both the saddle-bag and his horse missing. It had taken him an hour wandering around the wood before he ran to the village to raise the alarm. By that time Humphrey was a long way off, well on his way back to his familiar countryside. What could the collector say? He could not say that he had gone to sleep and lost the rental monies. So he had said that he had been attacked by a band of 6 or 7 murderous robbers armed to the teeth with knives and clubs. He had fought hard dealing with 2 or 3 of them but eventually he had been overwhelmed and the saddle-bag wrenched from his grasp. Fortunately the cuts and bruises he had sustained running wildly around the wood through the briars and shrubs added some credence to his story.

When the tale was told for the 3rd or 4th time the number of robbers had risen in number to nine or ten.

But when the local landowner and militia had ridden up to the scene of the ambush they could mysteriously find no sign of a struggle. The collector's horse was found quietly grazing in a nearby field, again with no signs of being involved in struggle of any kind.

At first the finger of suspicion was pointed at the rent collector himself, as no other rational explanation could be considered. But he stuck to his story about being attacked and none of the monies could be found. It was thought that the collector may have buried the saddle-bag in the woods. So the woods were scoured but nothing was ever found. Eventually the collector's story had to be accepted, despite no real evidence to sustain it.

For the rent collector himself he could come up with no earthly explanation. In his private thoughts he felt that a mysterious evil spirit or the devil himself had silently taken the saddle-bag leaving him the cloak as a threatening sign. He could not come up with any other reasonable explanation in his own mind.

At the 'Wolf's Head' a different tale was told about the incident, more along the lines of a gluttonous rent collector falling into a drunken stupor. This was the cause of much laughter and celebration, funded inadvertently by the rent collector himself. Much fun was had literally at his and his master's expense.

Over the next weeks and months Humphrey often rode out beyond Oswestry and into the Welsh hills. His horse became familiar with the tracks and pathways leading to and from the Meredith country estate. He even became a familiar figure to the farm dogs in the yard, who by now began to greet him like an old friend. This probably had something to do with his habit of bringing them a few choice tit-bits left over from his last meal or scrounged from the Landlord at the Wolf's Head.

Isabella was always waiting for him with open arms. She had acquired the habit of doing more for herself and thus not requiring the services of her chambermaid. Initially this seemed strange but in time was accepted by the maid, after all it meant less work. Sometimes Isabella would decide to have her supper sent to her room rather than join her mother and father. They just thought that she was a little tired or unwell.

Nothing could have been further from the truth. She was looking forward to a very active night and couldn't have felt better.

By the next morning she certainly did appear tired, confirming her parents concerns from the previous evening.

Humphrey made sure that he did not oversleep again, taking care to leave just before dawn. Cloaked in darkness he could creep away with ease.

He became a familiar sight in the surrounding villages as he passed through, but this merely confirmed him as a regular trader doing business with the merchant. Following the incident with the rent collector the militia stepped up their patrols in that area, but Humphrey decided not to operate on this patch as it may draw too much attention to his other night-time activities with Isabella. He returned to his usual haunts nearer to his home ground to allow the situation to cool down for a while.

Everything was fine on the Welsh borders as far as Humphrey was concerned. He could stand at the entrance to his cave and look out across his realm and feel very satisfied.

For Isabella it was a life of uncertainty, as she could never know when Humphrey would be next appearing. Sometimes they would plan for a certain night but something else would force Humphrey to change his plans and Isabella would be left waiting and longing. On other occasions he would appear out of the blue and she would have an overwhelming feeling of shock and elation as she heard the tap at her window.

It was now into summer and the nights were much lighter for longer. Welcomed by most these light nights were not altogether an asset to the highwayman. The darkness was often his friend and ally, allowing him to slip away into the woods to use his own local knowledge of the tracks and by-ways to evade any pursuers. The light nights made everything more even, nullifying the advantages of his knowledge and experience. He had to be more careful in his concealment, when planning an ambush, and he had to be more careful when planning his nightly escapades with Isabella.

As on other occasions the evening found Humphrey riding through the countryside of the Welsh border country. Due to the light skies there was still plenty of activity in the fields, with labourers harvesting the crops for the landowners. Some looked up as the rider trotted by but in general his passing did not cause any great interest, focussed as most of them were on the task in hand.

In the villages women were still going about their business outside and the children and dogs greeted the traveller in their own individual ways. Humphrey passed on through heading for the manor house where he intended to spend the night with Isabella. He rode his mare up and down the narrowing lanes until once again he reached the secluded spot, where he knew he could conceal his mare for the night. The lush green foliage of the summer months provided better cover than when he had first found this spot.

He climbed down from his mount and unsaddled her, allowing her to graze within the small copse. She was now familiar with the routine and knew that her master would not be back until the early hours of the morning.

Humphrey waited for a little time waiting for the sky to begin to dim as the sun eventually dropped down in the sky. He patted his mare one last time and whispered reassuringly in her ear, before stealthily following the hedge line towards the manor house and the prize within. He followed a familiar trail from one field to another keeping well hidden behind the lush growth of the summer hedges. As he approached the out-buildings he eyed the area for human activity. He felt in his pocket for the small paper parcel. Reassured he crept on into the yard. The dogs looked around but made no pretence of barking. Instead they trotted up hopefully. Humphrey made sure that they were not disappointed, opening up the paper parcel and laying out the pieces of meat and bone salvaged from one of his last meals. The dogs wagged their tails in appreciation and began to gobble up the morsels. Humphrey left them as they happily scoffed the gifts. Listening to the hubbub of noise from the kitchens he hurried across to the wall of the manor house and quickly leaped up to the flat roof, from where he knew he could traverse along the ledge to the window he was seeking. He kept flat to the wall in the growing darkness. He was just one more shadow. The shadow knocked on the wooden shutters and very soon afterwards they were opened from within. Isabella threw her arms around him and he reciprocated. They kissed long and hard. It had seemed an age since they were last able to meet. Quickly the shutters were closed behind the intruder to shut out the world and to shut in their own love tryst.

Isabella had taken some supper to her room in preparation for the meeting and after making love they both shared the supper.

"Are you able to stay the night, my love?" enquired Isabella full of hope.

"Tonight, definitely" came the welcome reply and Humphrey leaned over to kiss her once more. Isabella smiled in satisfaction and anticipation. They ate heartily, washed down with wine and then they fell to love-making again.

The morning arrived too soon again. The dawn came early in these light summer days and the morning light began to filter through the shutters into the warm sweet room, where the lovers lay. Isabella stirred.

"Humphrey, you must wake. It is morning already."

Although she did not want him to leave at all, she understood his need for speed and secrecy. Humphrey roused himself, kissed Isabella once more and began to dress himself. He reached over to eat the remains of last night's supper and washed it down with the dregs of the wine.

Throwing on his cape he leaned over one last time to give Isabella a lingering kiss.

"Until the next time, my dearest Isabella."

"Make it soon, my darling."

"I will try to make it next week. Wait for me!" Humphrey turned and tentatively peeped through the shutters at the scene outside. The sun was beginning to rise in the sky and the darkness was slowly turning more to an orange grey. Blowing one last kiss Humphrey crept through the window and began his steady traverse of the ledge. Keeping his ears open to the sounds of the household waking up he quickly retraced his steps from the night before and made his way past the out-buildings towards the greenery beyond. One or two of the sleepy dogs looked up but did not stir. Humphrey was clear away again.

He trekked back up the fields again keeping close to the hedge-line for concealment. In the half light and with all the foliage it would have taken a very keen eye indeed to have picked out a figure of any kind.

But on this one occasion that was precisely the situation.

"I see some-one coming, sir!" whispered one of the militia men excitedly. The officer hurried across.

"Where man? Where? I see nothing." He strained his eyes in the half light, squinting to try to focus better.

"It was over there, sir" whispered the militia man again, "over by that tall hedge." He pointed but nothing could really be seen.

"It was probably just another deer." Suggested one of the other militia men from behind. The small group of 6 men began to huddle around the officer and they all strained their eyes and ears in the early morning.

"Keep your voice down" retorted the officer. He was still hopeful of a successful mission in capturing the notorious highwayman, Humphrey Kynaston. He would, no doubt be rewarded handsomely and probably achieve a promotion as well. He felt honoured to have been picked by the Sheriff for this mission, to have the opportunity of furthering his career. He was taking this mission seriously. Besides he had a personal grudge to settle with the highwayman. The officer in command was Anthony Mytton. He wanted revenge for the incident when the merchant's carriage had been held up and he had been humiliated in front of his fiancé, Isabella.

The others were less enthusiastic, after having been up all night riding to this manor on the welsh border, having sat around in the dark for many hours, feeling cold and hungry and having been alerted to the movement of every deer and fox in the vicinity. Seeing nothing they returned to their positions sitting on tree stumps and logs, passing the time and looking forward to a hearty breakfast when all this was over.

"You keep watching. We will get this highwayman if it kills us" Whispered Mytton. The others overheard this and didn't particularly like the sound of the killing bit. They exchanged looks but thought it wise to say nothing.

The militia were acting on information from a local villager that a stranger, who resembled the description of the notorious highwayman, had been seen passing through the village and this was not the first time either. The villager was hoping for a slice of the reward money that had been posted.

The militia acting on this information had followed the route they had been told, which had led down the lane to the manor house of the rich merchant. The Sheriff imagined that the highwayman must have turned his hand to common thievery, deciding to rob from merchants' houses, perhaps because things were getting too dangerous on the highways due to the increased patrols.

They had decided to take the information seriously and put out a patrol to try to trap the highwayman. The sheriff knew that Mytton had a personal interest and decided that he was the best man for the job.

They had followed the track down to the main gate of the manor and had decided to set their trap outside the gate. So they lay in waiting amongst the hedgerows to the side of the track. They had now waited many hours and the initial enthusiasm and expectancy had by now worn off, except that is for Mytton.

"If he was here, he's long gone by now" muttered one of the men. "He would be in and out quick, woulden he?"

"Hold your tongue, man" snapped Mytton, still holding out hope for a successful mission, despite all the evidence suggesting that he had missed his prey, if he had ever been here.

Meanwhile oblivious to all that was going on at the gateway Humphrey had made his way up through the fields and had reached the secluded copse, where he had left his mare to overnight. She was reassured to see him and came trotting over to her master. He was reassured to see her also.

He patted her on the neck and she nuzzled into his chest.

Humphrey strolled over to the saddle and lifted it up easily onto the back of his mount. He fitted it securely, all the time whispering reassuringly to the mare and patting and stroking her. They were a team and relied on each other, that was clear. Feeling relaxed in the early morning, listening to the birds beginning their chorus, Humphrey pulled himself up onto his mount and they started on their way down the overgrown track back towards the main gate. Everything seemed just wonderful in the world from where he was sitting.

As they made their way along the track the mare became a little restless.

"What is it, my love?" He asked reassuringly, "There is nothing to worry us. Is it a fox, perhaps? Don't worry he will stay out of our way"

The mare carried on, but remained restless. She could smell the militia men and their horses and knew that this was not normal. She had been this way many times by now and there had never before been any other people or horses. But she was reassured that her master was in control and knew his business.

"What's that?" said a startled militia man. He had heard some movement in the bushes behind him and he turned to see the caped horseman trotting through the undergrowth.

"It's him!" He shouted "It's him. The highwayman."

Humphrey was shaken from his reverie, his horse whinnied in surprise. A shout went up from the militia men.

"He's there, he's there"

It was difficult to know who was the most surprised out of all the characters. For a moment nothing seemed to happen, as they all stood about taking in the sudden information.

Then they were suddenly galvanised, realising that this is what they were actually there for.

"Grab your weapons, men!" Ordered Mytton. "Get him. Don't let him get away!" He barked out these obvious orders, more in shock than in command.

A mad scramble ensued, with the men rushing around trying to locate their swords in the half light. Mytton was at the ready, sword in hand and standing directly in the centre of the track.

"Halt, highwayman, and give yourself up by the order of the Lord Sheriff of Shropshire." He bellowed out the command.

Humphrey, himself initially taken by surprise, had also been galvanised into action. Steadying himself on his horse he also had drawn his sword and being the only one mounted he charged forward meaning to break past the waiting soldiers. The militia men began to scatter as the horse bore down upon them, but the officer stood his ground.

"Halt, in the name of the Sheriff!" He shouted out again. He raised his sword as Humphrey came charging at him. He swung but he was met with Humphrey's blade, the force of which knocked him to the ground and the mounted highwayman galloped past and up the stony track leaving the militia men and their officer shouting and floundering behind. He galloped on wanting to put as much ground as possible between him and this skirmish. That had been close and he could feel the sweat of fear trickling down his neck and forehead. That had been too close.

The men rushed over to their officer and helped him to his feet. They now had their weapons to hand, just a little too late. He pulled himself up and shook off some of the mud. He was shocked but still determined.

"Quick, mount up! We must pursue him immediately. He will not get away from us this time."

The battle had now become even more personal.

The rest of the men looked a little bewildered and perplexed. They had been awake all night, were feeling cold and had been looking forward to a hearty hot breakfast. The last thing they wanted to do was to chase a notorious highwayman around the countryside.

"Come on, men. Lets mount up and be after the blaggard." Shouted Mytton, keen to capture his prize and the future promotion that beckoned. He was first to his horse. Quickly he mounted but had to wait impatiently while the rest of his men gathered their wits and their belongings, found their horses and mounted.

"Come on, he will be getting further away." Mytton urged his men on. They were less enthusiastic and secretly hoped that in fact the highwayman had got clean away.

Mytton dug his heels into his mount and away he rode. The others set off duty bound behind him.

They clattered into the first village, where people were rousing themselves for the days work ahead.

"You, man." Mytton called over to a labourer. "Did you see a rider pass this way and which way did he go?"

"Yes, sir. A rider passed by just a little while ago. He seemed in a great hurry. He headed out that way up over the brow." The labourer pointed and without a further word the officer charged on, his men followed. At the top of the brow Mytton called out excitedly, "There he is. I see him across those fields and heading up past that little patch of woodland. Quick we must not lose sight of him. We must stay on his trail."

Meanwhile at the other end of the chase Humphrey was urging his mare on to greater effort. He was not overly worried. He had a good, fast horse and a good head start. But he had to admit, that this time it had been too close for comfort. Had the militia been more alert he could easily have been captured or had to fight his way out of the situation. But he was away now and as before the militia would soon give up the chase. So he did not have too much to worry on that score. What worried him more was the fact that they had traced his movements to this part of the countryside and to the manor house where his beloved Isabella lived. How much did they already know?

His movements had obviously been noted more than he had imagined. Did they know about Isabella? Surely not.

These were the thoughts that were occupying his mind as he rode on along the road. As he approached a crossroads he strayed from the main road, preferring the smaller, narrower, less used track which cut up to the left and was more wooded and rugged. He knew all the tracks in this part of the world, as he had travelled them for many years learning all the short-cuts and hidden ways. Today was a day he was going to have to put his knowledge to its full use.

The group of militia approached the crossroads. They halted for a little while, as the officer pondered on which direction the highwayman had gone. He climbed down from his horse to inspect the ground.

"These seem to be the freshest hoof prints." He mused. "I think he must have left the main road to divert up this other track." His men offered no opinion. They were still hoping for a hot breakfast.

"This way then, men." He called as he remounted and started up the less used track. They had lost sight of the highwayman by now with all the rise and fall of the fields and the heavily leaved trees. It was fairly easy to be concealed at this time of year and in this sort of terrain. But Mytton seemed still to be positive and determined. He led the way up the track, by now at a slower pace, realising that they were not going to catch the highwayman quickly. He had resolved that this was going to be a steady pursuit involving tracking skills and good fortune.

Humphrey stopped when he felt he had outrun his pursuers. His mare needed to rest for a while. He turned and looked back. He could see nothing but fields and trees. He was confident that the militia were now on their way home and that he could relax a little. This incident had certainly taken him by surprise and seriously worried him. It was the connection with Isabella that most worried him. On one hand he was concerned for her safety but on the other worried that he would now find it increasingly difficult to continue this relationship with the woman he had fallen in love.

He turned his mare in the direction of the Nesscliffe. It would be a good half a day's ride before he arrived at his place of safety. He nudged her into a walk. But he had only gone another few minutes ride when he heard shouts from behind, which caused him to stop and look again. On the brow of the last hillock he spotted agitated figures on horseback. They had stopped also and were gesturing in his direction. His heart sank. It was the militia.

He was dumbstruck. He had not expected them to have continued the chase for so long. They were still some distance away, but they were clearly determined and had an added spur to their efforts on seeing their prey again. He turned his mare again.

"Sorry, old girl, no rest for us yet. We are in for another spell of hard riding."

He dug in his spurs and the mare responded gallantly again to the wishes of her master. They rode on at speed.

Behind him Humphrey could hear the cries of the militia caught on the breeze, as they also spurred their horses into a rapid pursuit.

At last he came in sight of the sandstone cliffs of this hideaway. They were surrounded by dense woodland on the steep slopes. 'Surely he would lose them in these woods' Humphrey tried to reassure himself.

He spurred his mare onwards eager to be engulfed by the thick greenery of the woodland. He did not dare stop. He had never been pursued in this way ever before. This was a new and worrying experience for Humphrey.

He had been riding since the early hours of the morning and now it was well into the evening. He had not been able to stop for food and only for a few minutes to take on water and to allow his mount to drink from the streams as they crossed them. But neither had the band of militia men halted for any length of time. The hot breakfast the men had looked forward to had long gone astray and they had been lucky to rush a meal of bread and cheese from an inn along the route.

He galloped into the woodland and immediately began to weave in and out of the trees and along the narrow paths that he and his mount knew well. He did not ride directly towards his hideaway, but instead decided on a circuitous route up the most difficult and inaccessible routes. He had to throw his pursuers off his trail before he was safe enough to slip into his cave hideaway. As he approached a particularly steep climb he quickly slid from his mount and led her up the roughly cut out steps. The light was beginning to fade now as the sun began to drop beyond the far side of the hill. It could not come soon enough for Humphrey. The darkness would be his friend and companion.

He knew these wooded pathways and hills like the back of his hand and was well used to travelling them by night time with only the moon to light the way. If he could keep the militia on the run until darkness fell, then he knew he would be safe. He remounted at the top of the slope and again galloped off down the winding tracks. The sweat had run down his neck and back, dried and then run again. It was cooler now as evening came but his exertion was no less. He stopped at the top of a slope, hidden amongst a copse of trees. He could not see his pursuers as the wood was dense. But he kept his mare as quiet as he could and listened intently.

The breeze rustled the leaves on the trees. A few birds called out going to roost. He listened again. His could hear the sound of his own breathing and the heavy breathing of his mare.

Straining his ears he could just catch the sound of some shouting and calling. It was way below him and the sound carried up to him. The militia were still down there but quite a long way away by the sound. He decided to dismount again, feeling a little safer. He still held the reins of his horse, ready to remount and gallop off again if he needed to.

He continued to strain his ears. The shouts drifted off and again he could hear nothing. Darkness had fallen by now and there was only a faint tinge of red on the horizon. It would soon be gone completely.

He waited long until his sweat was completely dry and he began to feel cold and shiver under the clear dark night sky. He had not heard a human sound for a good while now. The familiar sounds of the hill and forest comforted him. The occasional hoot or twit of an owl, the rustle as some small animal rummaged around in the leaf litter. He could distinguish these sounds from anything man-made. Eventually as the darkness completely engulfed the hill Humphrey felt safe enough to lead his horse along a different windy path back down from the plateau at the top of the hill, but he did not head all the way back down the hill. He still walked tentatively, stopping every now and again to listen for any foreign sounds. Each time he felt more reassured as he could hear nothing extraordinary.

He led his mare towards the vast impenetrable sand stone cliffs. But to him and his mare they were not impenetrable. Well hidden behind dense vegetation he located a fissure in the rock face that led through to his cave, his hideaway. He unsaddled his horse and rubbed her down with some of the straw which lay on the cave floor. He let her drink and feed, while he went out once again into the woodland. Retracing his steps along the path he used a small piece of foliage to brush away the tracks. Having camouflaged the entrance to the cave, he felt he could finally catch a bite to eat and much needed sleep. He ate some bread from his saddlebag.

It was a little dry and stale, certainly not what he was used to, but it tasted good under the circumstances. Although still concerned about the pursuit he was exhausted and fell asleep huddled in his cloak and blankets.

Darkness and the woodland had certainly been his friends and salvation. As the militia men continued to ride in hot pursuit the light had begun to fade. The horses and men were getting tired. Undeterred Mytton had pressed his men to carry on for the glory of capturing the notorious highwayman and the rewards they would all come by. And he would have any man flogged if they didn't. But as they reached the edge of the wood and darkness fell, even his resolve began to fade. He tried to urge his men to continue the pursuit, but this was their limit. They were not going to persist into the darkness and unknown, to be at the mercy of a blood thirsty outlaw, who could pick them off one by one. Not only that there was no way they could track him in the dark. How could they distinguish hoof marks or broken twigs in pitch black? As the sounds of the night forest flourished around them they began to imagine ghosts and strange creatures that lurked in the darkness. All the local legends of monster wolves or bears or other mysterious creatures flooded their minds. The owls hoot became the cry of an evil spirit, the rustle of a hedgehog a poisonous serpent and the toe curling howl of a dog fox a wild banshee. This was all too much for the reluctant militia men, fed only on bread, cheese and water.

Reluctantly Mytton had to admit defeat and wave goodbye to his reward. He too did not relish following the wolf into his own lair, especially not at night.

They had turned away from the hill, turning their backs on the threatening woodland and headed towards civilisation, food, warmth and sleep.

Chapter Nine

Humphrey woke early as usual. The sweat felt dry and cold on his skin. He began to sweat again just remembering the events of the previous day and night. He could not allow himself to be complacent. He had escaped once again but this time the pursuit had become perilously close. Much too close for any comfort. They had chased him and tracked him to the very doorstep of the hideaway that had kept him safe all these years. They probably had not known how close they had been to running him to ground, but Humphrey knew and it worried him.

He rose, quickly throwing some water over his face to fully revive him. His horse sensing his presence snorted. She had at least rested well and eaten. He still felt bedraggled and hungry.

"We must ride again, my beauty." He whispered soothingly to her. "You served me well last night but we are not clear yet."

He quickly saddled her up and once more before first light the pair were on their way. The mare was well used to these early morning outings by now. Carefully brushing their way through the camouflage they headed down the steep slope and away from the protection of the wall of sandstone.

Humphrey felt that the militia may return to try to pick up the trail from the night before. He felt he could not take the chance of remaining in his hideaway when the militia had come so close. He headed off to his other familiar haunts to seek refuge amongst the underclass of thieves and robbers, with whom he had associated. He would seek out his brother Thomas and Hopton, who could give him refuge for a while. He knew he would have to be very cautious and tread warily for the coming weeks. On this occasion he chose to keep a low profile and his greatest sadness was that he could not dare to visit his beloved Isabella for fear of capture. This was one time in his life when bravado was not the order of the day.

Fortune shined on Humphrey even if the weather over the next few days did not. To Humphrey's advantage it rained the next day. It meant that he got wet but more importantly it washed away any tracks from around his hideout amongst the sandstone caves. The militia had not been organised enough to come out the next day as they had been exhausted after their days forced pursuit. They all had other occupations and duties that also needed attending to. So it was two days later before Mytton and his men could return to search the hills for their prey. By this time all track and trace of the highwayman had been obscured. They scoured the hill but without any success. By this time Humphrey was well away from the area and in hiding.

Mytton had to give up not only on the pursuit of the highwayman but also on the promotion he had pursued.

Tales of the great pursuit and escape abounded in the various inns. The reputation of the highwayman continued to increase. For once Humphrey was not altogether pleased with this. He was trying to keep a lower profile. He needed the dust to settle, for him to return to visiting his beloved Isabella. It was just too dangerous to begin his nightly escapades again. The merchant, Isabella's father, had employed some extra guards at his property and the militia were much more active in the area, Mytton still hoping to gain some success and pick up some leads. Twice humiliated he did not intend to give up now.

Isabella had heard from her father about the great chase and the fact that the highwayman had been in such close proximity to their property. He imagined the highwayman had been plotting to rob him again, but he could hardly believe the audacity of the man. He had ordered an armed presence to be set up around his manor to deter any such further plans. Mytton himself gave his personal assurance that he would see to the protection of the property and the safety of his fiancé. Isabella guessed that Humphrey would be forced to lie low under these circumstances, but breathed a sigh of relief that he had again escaped his pursuers. But she also missed her lover greatly and wondered at how long it would be before she could see him again. Every night she kept her shutters ever so slightly ajar, just in case he were to appear. Her maids were always keen to close the shutters but Isabella said that she needed the fresh air for her health and they reluctantly deferred.

Humphrey lay low. He tended to stay indoors at his brother's house during the day and ventured out under cover of darkness to visit his old haunts and dens of thieves. Sometimes he would stay over at the less salubrious abode of Hopton. He did not want his habits or movements to become too predictable. He felt he could no longer altogether trust the band of thieves amongst whom he lived. Someone had betrayed him to the militia to set up the trap and he needed to become more wary.

He no longer engaged in his old pastimes as readily as before. His mind and heart were elsewhere. Perhaps he was getting a little old for the life and antics of a highwayman.

He was approaching the Wolf's Head one late afternoon and on spotting a small gathering outside the inn, he reined back his mare to view the scene from some small distance.

A Sheriff's man was mounted in the midst of the ragged and hoary band.

The men, mostly dirty, unshaven, many with scars or other abominable features, simply stood or sat staring at the smart figure on his smart horse. They were silent except for a few murmurs of suspicion. To the horseman it seemed a threatening silence. He noted the knives and swords hanging from the ruffians' waists and rested his hand on his own sword in anticipation.

He had passed under the sign where a wolf's head snarled ferociously down at him. The men seemed to be snarling at him also. The horseman had reined up outside the inn door and gingerly leaving the hilt of his sword pulled from his saddlebag a notice. Without dismounting for fear of assault he leaned across to the doorpost and nailed up the notice. His duty done he turned his horse around and trotted off back down the track. Reaching a bend a few hundred yards away he halted to breath a sigh of relief. He looked back seeing the men at the inn hustling around the notice he had just posted. The relieved deputy then rode on out of sight and into safety.

Humphrey watched the man ride away before approaching the inn. He guessed that it was another reward poster, presumably with an increased price on his head. All the more reason for him to be wary. Any small time thief or ruffian might be tempted to give information on him in exchange for a fat purse.

As he rode closer he could hear the hubbub and murmur from the small crowd. As his mare trotted into view some were already returning inside to quench their thirst or to their gambling. A few turned their heads as they heard his approach, but on recognising Kynaston they turned back to their murmurings.

The bear like figure of Hopton stepped from the crowd.
"What is it? More money on my head?" Asked Kynaston.

"Not this time." Came a muffled noise from the great beard. "It's about war with France!"

Humphrey dismounted. This was indeed something new and newsworthy. He pushed through the diminishing crowd to read better the official notice. Hopton followed him. As Hopton had said it was an announcement of a forthcoming campaign to be led by the King himself to engage in battle with France to reclaim lands justly belonging to the English Crown.

By proclamation of Henry VIII himself all honourable knights and followers were urged to come forward to take on the enemy.

"That is quite some news." Humphrey spoke out loud but mainly to himself. He stood reading the notice over again. By this time only Kynaston and Hopton were left outside the inn. All the rest had returned indoors to their other activities.

"Lets go inside and have a drink, my old friend." Kynaston led the way. Hopton had to stoop as he followed.

"Drinks all around, for all my good friends." He immediately announced as he entered the darkness inside. He tossed a bag of coins onto the counter to the landlord.

"Set up the drinks, landlord!"

A cheer went up from the rabble as they quickly drank up and rushed up for a refill courtesy of the local highwayman and legend.

"I thought that you were keeping your head down." Whispered Hopton."

"True, true, my old friend. But I still need to buy myself some friends and goodwill. Besides I have a feeling that things are about to change and that new adventures are once again ahead of us."

Hopton looked at Kynaston, bewildered at this sudden change of mood. Kynaston took up his own drink and threw himself into the throng.

CHAPTER TEN

KING HENRY HAD declared a war on France and needed to recruit an army from among the noblemen of England. He needed knights and other worthy experienced fighting men to take on the French King to reclaim the lands of Northern France.

Kynaston saw not only the opportunity for adventure and riches but also a chance of salvation. With the recent narrow escape Kynaston felt that his life as a highwayman was beginning to carry too many risks. It had of course always been a risky occupation, but he had never really cared that much about his own safety. But now he felt he had something and someone he wanted to live for. His love for Isabella had given him something he did not want to lose. But clearly he could not continue the relationship and maintain his life beyond the law. It would only be a matter of time before he was trapped, captured or his hideout located.

The feud with Mytton had become personal and only one of them could survive. Kynaston had come to this realisation since the chase and in the instant that he had seen the notice regarding the war with France a possible plan had begun to form.

Over the next few days he visited his brother, Thomas at the family home to get his opinion on the plan that he had conceived. He invited Hopton along to a meeting and all three of them sat down to a long deliberation under the cover of darkness. Over a few glasses of good French wine they talked long into the night. Finally they stood up together and solemnly shook hands on the decision they had agreed. They then slunk off to bed.

The next morning both Humphrey Kynaston and Hopton rose early to be on their way. Humphrey was still being very cautious following the chase and did not want to be found near the house of his brother. They both collected their horses from the stable and surveying the scene in the half light headed out through one of the side entrances to the estate, which had been kept purposely semi-overgrown for this very reason of secrecy. There was the possibility that militia men were keeping an eye on the main entrance just in case he were to appear. Humphrey was taking no chances. The odd couple warily weaved their way along the narrow, overgrown track keeping their ears and eyes sharp to any strange noises or happenings. They trotted on and were soon away from the estate and heading for the Wolf's Head where they would get some breakfast and await word from Thomas.

Later Thomas gathered himself together and having breakfasted well had his horse saddled and set out through the main gates heading for the County town. He was dressed in his most formal clothes and rode out on a mission. By midday Thomas had reached Shrewsbury, the County town. He approached over the very bridge where years earlier Humphrey had jumped for his life and swam the river to elude the guards at the gates. Thomas was clearly a worthy gentleman and had no trouble in gaining access over the bridge and to the town. He turned sharply to the North and headed for the castle. He rode steadily without hesitation. The sandstone edifice of the castle came into view as he rode closer. He continued on his way riding up to the entrance. Here he was challenged by the guards as to his name and as to his business at the castle.

"Thomas Kynaston." He replied with no hesitation. "I have come to have an audience with the Sheriff. Please convey to him my wish to speak with him on a matter of great importance."

One of the guards duly trotted off towards the inner buildings, while Thomas remained seated on his horse awaiting his audience. Five minutes later the guard came running back with two other guards with the message that the Sheriff was having lunch but would welcome Thomas Kynaston and invited him to join him. The guards stepped aside and Thomas nudged his mount to walk on. They passed through the red sandstone archway and into the grounds inside. Thomas took the track to the left leading to the interior buildings, where the Sheriff held court when in the county town. Thomas pulled up outside the main door and dismounted. His horse was held by the stablehand, who took it off to the stables for food and rest. Thomas was greeted by a squire and ushered through doorway to a hall beyond.

The Sheriff was dining with a few wealthy local landowners, having been discussing business affairs.

"Ah, welcome Thomas Kynaston. Please join us, won't you! I must say I have not often had the pleasure of conversation with you and I am curious as to your business. But, first have some food and drink."

Thomas acquiesced and indulged in some food but took great care not to partake of the wine. He needed to keep a clear head in his dialogue with the Sheriff.

When every one was well satiated from the meal the landowners said their farewells and departed.

"You require a private audience, I believe." Remarked the Sheriff.

"That is correct." Replied Thomas, "I have an important proposal to discuss with you."

They retired to a side room, where they could have more privacy. The Sheriff closed the door behind them and the dialogue began.

When they emerged about an hour later the table had been cleared and a servant was sweeping the floor. Thomas picked up his cloak and turned to the Sheriff. They shook hands and parted. A servant was sent to the stable and Thomas went outside to await his horse.

It was early afternoon and the sun shone high in the sky. It felt a bright auspicious day.

A few minutes passed as Thomas soaked up the sun. He turned as he heard the steady clip-clop of his horse as it was led from the stable. Thomas swung himself up into the saddle and trotted towards the sandstone archway through which he had entered a few hours earlier. Again the guards stepped aside as he approached and soon he was back out into the hustle and bustle of the busy town streets.

He felt relieved and content. It had gone to plan. By that evening he could be back at his family mansion, where after dark he could expect to be visited by two cloaked men, eager to hear his words.

Humphrey and Hopton had spent the day between one inn and another, merely passing the day idly in playing games and in conversation. But neither had over-indulged with drinking and both seemed pre-occupied. This had been remarked on by a few of their associates,

"Keep yer mind on the game, will yer!" snarled one.

"A woman on yer mind, I reckon." joked another.

Humphrey raised his hand in apology and excused himself from the card game.

"I think I need some fresh air." He stood up and went outside. About five minutes later Hopton joined him and they fell into conspiratorial conversation. They were both wondering how Thomas was faring on his mission to the Sheriff. For them the evening could not come soon enough, when they would be able to hear the result of the negotiations.

"This could be our last chance, my old friend." Mused Humphrey "We are both getting a little long in the tooth for roaming the highways. I feel the time has come to make some more permanent plans. I cannot live forever in a hideaway on the hillside."

His friend merely nodded. Hopton was a man of few words. But each understood the importance of the moment. After a period of thoughtful silence Hopton gestured back towards the door of the Inn. Humphrey nodded and they both returned to the fray inside, again to pass the time until nightfall, when they could ride out to visit Thomas and hear his news.

Thomas had returned to his manor house and was eagerly awaiting his visitors. Once under darkness he heard a knock on the door and quickly answered the door himself.

"Come on in Humphrey, Robert. We have much to discuss. Come through to the dining room." Thomas led the way.

They stood at the table, which was laid with some cold meats, bread and cheese. Ale was in a jug. Humphrey helped himself to a drink and gestured to Hopton, who with a nod acknowledged his mutual desire.

"Well, Thomas, what is the news? Are we to drink to the future or are we to drown our sorrows?" Asked Humphrey directly.

The Highwayman's Cave

Thomas paused for a few seconds before beginning with his momentous news.

"Good news, my friends. So fill your tankards and I will tell you all."

"Hurrah!" Shouted Humphrey. Hopton raised his tankard and they all clinked their tankards in camaraderie.

"Tell us all, Thomas, and do not spare any details."

In between several fillings of their tankards and much questioning Thomas proceeded to relate how he had met with the reluctant Sheriff and put forward their proposal. How the Sheriff had listened intently and had many doubts over which he needed reassurance. He had questioned Thomas in depth about the proposal and how after much thought and negotiation an agreement had been made. The details of which he would lay before them:

As they had known the King was embarking on a war against France to secure lands and wealth in Northern France, which the King felt he had due rights to. For such a campaign the King requested and required the services of all noblemen of the country, especially those skilled and experienced in the art of warfare. With them they would bring their yeomen, servants and other young men of their area to form the basis of the army.

The proposal that Humphrey and Thomas put forward was for them to volunteer to fight for King and country in exchange for a free pardon on their return. The Sheriff had at first been very sceptical about the idea, with much good reason for doubting the word of a highway robber of such renown, who had caused him personally much concern and trouble over many years. But as the conversation flowed along with the wine kindly purchased by Thomas, the Sheriff could see the advantages to himself. He was commissioned by the Kings' authority to raise as many recruits as possible and would clearly be judged by his success or failure in this respect. Thomas Kynaston, Humphrey Kynaston and their accomplice Robert Hopton were clearly of a very fine fighting calibre and had more experience with weapons than most. Over the years they had clearly been a very sharp and painful thorn in his side and their exploits had caused him much embarrassment and shame within higher circles. To have them as his legitimate recruits fighting a war in France for their King would clearly be preferred to having them marauding around the countryside. The best gamekeepers are to be recruited from poachers. Indeed it might be seen as a feather in his cap if the Sheriff could at one stroke deal with the outlawry in his territory and furnish the King with such experienced and established fighting men. At the very least they would be otherwise occupied in a foreign land for some considerable time, perhaps they may even meet their death in the service of their King. Either way that would improve the Sheriff's lot immeasurably. What they wanted in return was a pardon from their past crimes.

If they did not return then he had nothing to lose. If they performed well for the King, that could only be another feather in the Sheriff's cap, and he could expect due reward in time. He would be able to take all the credit for the plan. As long as they did not return to their life of crime and highway robbery, the Sheriff did not feel he had much to lose. For this he accepted the word of Thomas Kynaston. And so a deal had been struck.

They would need to take the pledge to King and country, raise as many young men to go with them on the promise of wealth and glory to be gained and they could begin their path to legitimacy and freedom.

Humphrey and Hopton had listened intently to every detail that spilled from Thomas' lips hanging on every word, themselves questioning in the same way as had the Sheriff, with their own doubts and need for reassurance. But by the end there seemed nothing else to do but to once again raise their tankards in celebration and merriment. A sombre silence befell after Thomas' speech. They each sat down quietly taking in the gravity of the moment. This could mark such a great change in their lives. It was an opportunity that would not present itself again. They looked in unison at each other, nodded and once again raised their tankards in a toast to the King and to the future.

Chapter Eleven

Humphrey looked back towards the coast of England as it drifted away. It was a strange feeling. He had always been rather a land based creature and the experience on the sea was not altogether to his liking. He had been assured that it would be a short journey of less than a day. He was not looking forward to this crossing. He felt strange in another way also. He was amongst his peers, other nobles who had come forward to take up the King's call to arms. He was no longer the outsider. He was expected to play the role of an officer in the army and to socialise with his fellow officers and noblemen. He had always rejected their life and their ideas. He had preferred the life of revelry and mixing with the common people. This new role was artificial to him. It was frowned on by his fellow officers when he was seen speaking with the common soldiers. Hopton was Humphrey's right hand man but was looked down on with derision and suspicion by the noblemen. But on the other side Humphrey was respected by his men both due to his reputation and to the more casual way he was able and willing to talk to them. He treated them with respect and in turn received it from them.

Hopton came up behind him.

"I hope the horses will be alright." He grunted. "I don't think they were made to go to sea."

"I feel much the same myself, Robert." Replied Humphrey.

"You should call me Hopton. Remember."

Humphrey nodded reluctantly accepting the social rules. "While no one is listening, I would rather things were as they used to be back in the Wolf's Head."

"But we are not." Hopton replied bluntly. Again Humphrey nodded in acceptance. He watched the coastline slowly dipping over the horizon and thought of Isabella.

"I'm going below to sleep. Can't stand this rocking." Blurted Hopton. Humphrey looked over at his large bearded friend and could see that he looked a bit pale and green. He had only ever seen his friend like this after a batch of bad beer and even then very rarely, his capacity for drink being renowned.

"Mmm, good idea! We will need our strength for the days ahead." Replied Humphrey. "I think Thomas has already gone for a rest. I will stay here awhile, I think. I will check on the horses later."

Hopton nodded and gratefully sloped away. Humphrey remained up on the deck enjoying the breeze and looking back at the sun as it also began to sink beyond the horizon to join his homeland. He looked forward to the great adventure ahead and to the chance of a new life. But some memories connected him closely with the green hills and forests of the Welsh border country, where he had spent most of his life. He missed them greatly but mostly he missed the woman he loved who lived amongst those hills. As the sun dropped lower and the sky darkened Humphrey turned to go below, firstly to check on his trusty mare, before retiring to his chamber. As he turned, a familiar figure stood before him. At first Humphrey did not recognise him but the same was not true from the other party. Mytton stood before him, with two of his fellow officers.

"I had not realised that the Kings' army was so desperate as to take the likes of thieves and cheats." Mytton spoke as an aside to his companions, but clearly for Humphrey to hear. "You had better watch your back out here, Kynaston. There are no woods to hide amongst or thieves to protect you."

Humphrey recognised the arrogant voice he had heard in the Lion.

"We are here to fight the French, I believe, not to fight amongst ourselves." Replied Humphrey. "I need to pass to go below, if you will excuse me. I feel the air has suddenly gone chill above deck."

"You may have fooled the Sheriff, Kynaston, but you cannot fool me. I know a wolf in sheep's clothing. And I will look forward to the pleasure of shearing your fleece." Mytton laughed as did his companions. Humphrey pushed passed them and headed below.

The ship had anchored off the French coast overnight on arriving. As the light of day came around everyone seemed eager to disembark and touch again the solid ground, even if it was foreign ground. There was much to be done, with great activity in unloading supplies, horses and men. Everyone took their part in the great escapade and when everyone and everything had disembarked the camp was set up and celebrations were started. The first step of the great adventure had been accomplished. Feelings in the camp were high and confident.

Some weeks later they marched on Therouanne. The army led by Charles Brandon, had surrounded the town and laid siege to it. For weeks the English army stayed encamped around the town, hoping to slowly wear down the resolve of the townspeople. King Henry had amassed an army of 30,000 for his grand escapade and intended to gain great victories, wealth and honour through the campaign. Humphrey and his companions had initially been excited by the prospect of battle and glory, but as the time went on they had become less so. The realities of war seemed to bring a much more boring prospect than Humphrey had anticipated. To begin with the army had been occupied with marching, setting up and breaking camp and then setting up camp again.

For Humphrey these were not what he had been looking forward to. He did not enjoy the weight of command and left most of the organising of his troops to his lesser officers.

In the evenings he was obliged to share the company of his fellow officers. They engaged in playing cards and other games as well as drinking and eating heartily. As much as Humphrey normally would have enjoyed these activities, the company was not of his choosing. He would much rather have been enjoying the cut and thrust of the pastimes of the lower orders. He was envious of Hopton, who could move freely throughout the camp mixing with whoever he wanted. Humphrey on the other hand was expected to play the role of an officer and not to mix socially with his inferiors.

He grew easily bored of his fellow officers. Thomas Kynaston, on the other hand, seemed to fit more easily into their society and was able to bridge the gap between Humphrey and the officers.

The days were warm and the evenings light until late. There was a familiar smell that followed the army wherever they travelled. For the lower orders the numerous cesspits and lack of bathing water were commonplace and much as they experienced at home. But for the noblemen the smell was not to their liking. The inconveniences of an army on the march did not suit their sensibilities and idea of order.

Humphrey soon gained a reputation of being somewhat of a loner and an outsider. With his troops he was respected as a fair commander and an expert with sword and lance. Humphrey enjoyed nothing more than the practice sessions and fights between the officers and other noblemen. Humphrey was bested by no other man and the other officers gave him a begrudging respect when it came to battle skills.

But away from these organised skirmishes Humphrey seemed distracted. He was obliged to have his meals with the other officers of his class but his mind was always elsewhere. When not otherwise occupied his mind would drift to the hills of the Marches and the beautiful woman who lived there.

Unlike many of the other noblemen who had joined the campaign, he was not here particularly for wealth and glory. He had his mind focussed on the aftermath and the pardon that he will have earned.

Each day became the same routine of checking the troops, hearing any reports of activity from the town from the overnight guards. Humphrey had to deal with any misdemeanours or squabbles from amongst his men. He would listen to these accusations of drunkenness, thievery and fighting. He would then leave it to Hopton to administer any punishment or justice required. Normally following such justice the miscreants would know better than to cause trouble again.

One warm August morning Humphrey arose as usual but he was immediately summoned to a counsel in the Kings tent. He dressed quickly and strode off, but not in any great anticipation. These counsels had been held before whenever the King felt he had some great news to pronounce, but usually they had not amounted to anything of great significance. So Humphrey was not unusually excited.

"What's the tale, Humphrey?" Hopton caught up with Humphrey on the way to the King's tent.

"Just another meeting and pronouncement, I suppose." Came back Humphrey's bored reply. "I wish something would happen. I do not think that I can take much more of this tedium."

"Ah, well, let us know if out is 'appening. I could do with some action." Hopton backed off as Humphrey joined the other noblemen and officers rushing to the King's tent. Humphrey pushed his way into the back of the tent. It was already full by the time he had reached it.

"Humphrey, you are late." Rebuked Thomas, "This is serious, something is going on!"

The nobles and officers waited in anticipation as they waited for King Henry and his ministers to enter. There was a deferent hush as the King entered. This time unusually there was much less pomp and ceremony, the King made a short rousing speech and handed over to Charles Brandon, commander of the King's armies. Although Humphrey could not hear clearly from the back of the tent the information quickly was spread.

"The French are moving, Humphrey." Blurted the astonished and excited Thomas, "They are gathering a force a few miles to the south of the town in readiness to attack. This is it.! We are to make ready immediately and ride out to meet them."

All of a sudden the nobles and officers showed a great sense of urgency and were rushing back to their own tents to inform their own men and make them ready. Hopton came up to Humphrey on his way back.

"What is it, 'umphrey? What's going on?"

"At last it is time for action, Robert. Get the men ready! We are to meet the French in battle this day."

Hopton beamed, "This is our big chance, 'umphrey."

"It is so, Robert. So let us make the most of it and show the French the mettle of the English army."

They rushed back to their camp and announced to the gathered troops that they should make ready for battle immediately. Cheers went up from all around the camp as the men heard of the news and immediate steps were taken to make ready for battle.

The King's system of spies and lookouts had worked well. Advance notice of the impending French attack proved vital in allowing time for the English army to mass in preparation. The English army mustered and marched to meet the French forces. The prior knowledge of the French action allowed the English to be prepared and await the attack.

Humphrey, Hopton alongside him, waited hidden in woodland, with their men armed and ready.

"Just like old times, eh, Hopton?" Humphrey joked, "Waiting for the carriage to pass the old Ness Cliffe."

That same old excitement and anticipation was running through his blood again. They were ready for this. Some of the men, however, were not accustomed to fighting or warfare. This was their first and for some possibly their last battle. They waited silently saying prayers to their Lord and Maker, thinking of their families and loved ones back at home and wondering whether they would ever see them again. Many were visibly fearful, pale and shaking. Humphrey rode to the front confident and steady.

"Fear not, good fellows." Humphrey spoke clearly and calmly. "We go today to fight for our glory. Hold your heads up with honour and respect. We will soon be home to boast of our victory to our families and friends. Follow me now into battle with no fear and we will have the French on the run in no time."

Shortly the French army appeared advancing and the cry for attack went up from English and the battle began. Humphrey led his men from the front, leading by example, exuding confidence and demonstrating courage in his battle-skills. The English army descended on the French forces, who were taken somewhat by surprise. The French were immediately on the back foot. They had anticipated having the element of surprise, not the other way around.

The armies crashed with terrible noise and affray. Humphrey led gallantly lashing out to the left and to the right claiming French lives with every blow. His years of highway villainy had stood him in good stead for this moment. Hopton followed closely behind, his colossal figure striding through the enemy ranks taking all before him. Humphrey's men viewing this could not help but be spurred on in courage and took the fray to the French force.

All along the line the English army had the initiative. Finally Charles Brandon in the name of King Henry, led the charge of the mounted cavalry into the middle of the French force, who were already in disarray. They crashed through the front line of the French force leaving dead and wounded everywhere and charged on to engage the French Knights.

As the English clashed with them the French Knights fought bravely but were soon overwhelmed by numbers. Humphrey and Thomas on horseback were rushing up to join the charging cavalry, Hopton and the rest of his troops were following. As they viewed the scene of disarray and the oncoming English cavalry the French Knights did not have the stomach to continue the battle. The remainder of the knights turned their horses around and spurred on their mounts in retreat and total disarray. The cavalry set off in pursuit. Humphrey and his men came to a halt. The French army was now in total retreat and a huge cheer went up from the English army in absolute victory.

That night following the victory saw great celebrations in the English camp. Much wine and beer was consumed by the victorious English Army. Humphrey enjoyed himself alongside everyone else. This was reminiscent of his escapades back in Shropshire and the celebrations that usually followed in the Wolf's Head. He joined his men in ribaldry and celebration. They had been in this together and were going to celebrate together.

In some circles this behaviour mixing with the common soldiers was frowned upon but most of the nobles were themselves so intoxicated that they hardly noticed. But one particular officer was taking notice. Anthony Mytton had also joined up when King Henry had been seeking volunteers. He had been keeping his eye on Humphrey Kynaston throughout the few months of this campaign, making notes of his social misdemeanours and errors. At first he had reported them to his superiors, but they were generally ignored. Due to his fighting prowess some allowance was made for Humphrey and generally Mytton's complaints were ignored. But nevertheless Mytton kept up his observations waiting for a slip from his adversary, waiting for an opportunity for revenge. Ever since the embarrassments of the Lion Inn and the highway robbery, Mytton had been determined to seek his revenge. He had lost the betrothal of Isabella through this villain and was intent on nothing short of the death of Humphrey Kynaston.

Now was his chance.

Mytton watched as Humphrey moved amongst his soldiers conversing with them easily and naturally. There were many great whoops of laughter and merriment as he wandered through the throng of merry-makers. Hopton was demonstrating his huge capacity for ale and challenged anyone to drink him under the table or to wrestle. One or two had already taken up the challenge to their detriment, so on this occasion there were no takers and his prowess was allowed to go unchallenged. Humphrey laughed at his friend's antics.

"No man is stupid enough to take you on, Robert. Wait till you have drunk some more and I will take you myself." He joked.

"Or till _you_ have drunk some more!" Returned Hopton in good spirit.

"I will make room for some more." Replied Humphrey and he moved away from the revelry to the surrounding bushes in the darkness. He needed to relieve himself.

Mytton had been watching and now made his move. He quickly moved around the drunken revelry towards the very same bushes. But Mytton intended more than relief. Humphrey had turned to come back to the camp when Mytton jumped out in front of him sword in hand.

"Kynaston, you are mine. Meet thy maker." He swung at Humphrey, who howsoever under the influence of wine and beer, instinctively stepped to the side. But not quick enough as the sword sliced at his arm. The pain was temporarily held at bay by the alcohol but the blood told Mytton that he had hit home.

"No one will find your body until the morning and the French will be blamed." He advanced again swinging the sword ahead of him. Humphrey was unarmed, not feeling that he needed his weapon amongst his own men. The blood running from his arm seemed to shock him into sobriety. He span away but again Mytton hit home, catching him on his side.

"You will not escape me this time, Kynaston. I have waited a long time for this moment." Humphrey had slumped onto one knee as he felt weak and shocked. Mytton came in once more sensing his victory. This time Humphrey leapt forward and took Mytton in the chest, knocking him over and for a while they both rolled about in the dust. Mytton managed to pull away and once again raised up his sword for a final blow. Humphrey knocked Mytton's legs from under him and they both went rolling down a small mound into the ditch.

Hopton, on hearing the noise of fighting, burst through the bushes dagger in his hand.

"Wot's going on? Umphrey, where are you? Are you alright?" He rushed around trying to see what was happening in the darkness.

He heard the sound of a scuffle in the ditch below followed by the scream of pain. He had heard that sound often earlier that day during the heat of battle. It was the sound of death.

He leaped down the bank, "The French are upon us!"

Behind him the sound of singing and merriment ceased. Soldiers grabbed their weapons and rushed through the bushes to hunt the French attackers. But below him Hopton could see the figure of only one man. He leapt towards him determined that another Frenchman would die tonight on his blade.

"Hold!" came a weak voice. Something in the voice seemed familiar. Hopton hesitated only for a moment, but just long enough for the figure to gasp, "Robert, it is I, Humphrey." The figure collapsed.

Hopton gathered up his dear friend in his bear-like arms. He carried him up to camp calling to the soldiers for assistance. He was led to the officers' tent, where he laid Humphrey on a table. Someone ran off to get the physician. Others ran off to pursue the French scouting party.

Hopton was hustled out of the officers' tent as the physician arrived.

"You save him or else!" shouted Hopton. He rushed back to the scene of the fight to tackle the French cowards who had done this to his dear friend.

"Where are they? I'll kill them all."

"They must have run off, when they heard you." Spoke one soldier, "We've looked around but we have only found one body and we think he is ours."

Hopton leaped down to the ditch where the soldier was pointing. One soldier was carrying a lantern and he held it over the ditch. Hopton stared down at the body of a man he recognised as that of Anthony Mytton, his blood mingling with the mud of the ditch.

"Those cowardly French have done for this one. He is past saving." Muttered the lamp holder.

"Aye, that must be wot 'appened." Mumbled Hopton, "And then they got clean away."

"Must 'ave. No sign of them when we came."

"Take him back to his tent and set the guards to watch for more attacks." Ordered Hopton. His words carried authority and the soldiers duly obeyed.

Hopton returned to the officers' tent, where he had left Humphrey in the hands of the physician. He mulled over the news he had just witnessed. Thomas Kynaston was just coming out as Hopton arrived. The news from the physician was that although Humphrey had lost quite a lot of blood, his wounds should not be life threatening and that given time and rest he should recover. They would not let Hopton in to see Humphrey but Thomas had been allowed in and he was able to re-assure Hopton that Humphrey was going to be fine.

"He has survived wounds in the past. He will surely fight these off the same way. Do not worry Hopton. He will be back to his fighting self in no time."

Hopton beckoned for Thomas to follow him to a quiet spot. Thomas did so, curious as to what he was to hear. Hopton told him about Mytton being dead and the mystery of the French attack. They whispered amongst themselves.

"Let it be understood that he was killed by the French and we will say no more about it. Agreed, Robert?"

"Aye, that sounds about right." Hopton acknowledged.

CHAPTER TWELVE

HUMPHREY KYNASTON WAS quickly able to make a full recovery from his wounds, but he was not able to play any further part in the campaign against the French. The battle became known as the Battle of the Spurs in ridicule of the manner in which the French knights had turned and spurred on their horses in escape. Five days later the townspeople of Therouanne could hold out no longer and surrendered their town. The English marched on and soon took the further town of Tournai, which fell after only a few days of siege.

The English army could return home in victory. The nobles would be rewarded with lands and plundered wealth. The common soldiers had to plunder what they could. Humphrey Kynaston, Thomas Kynaston and Robert Hopton looked forward to claiming their own special reward on their return to England. For their valiant escapades on behalf of King Henry they were duly rewarded with the pardon they had bargained for and could return to Shropshire with honour as free men.

The leaves were beginning to turn crimson and russet in the autumn air. But the sun shone through the clouds and kept the chill at bay. It would be cool when the sun went down. The figure clad in black cloak rode along the highway. He rode a dark black mare. They made their way steadily along familiar roads and lanes through the countryside of the Welsh Marches. The figure rode steadily and purposefully.

He rode over a brow and down a slope towards a small river. A solid rustic wooden bridge allowed for easy crossing. It was not at all ornate but had clearly been designed to allow for the safe passage of carriages and carts. The road itself was basic but again wide enough for carriages. The horse's hooves pounded on the thick wooden beams as they crossed and soon after they came to the large gates, which announced the entrance to the merchant's manor. The tracks of the carriages could easily be seen in the muddy track as they turned through the gates and upwards towards the fine manor house nestling between the trees at the end of the long drive. Beyond the gates the road narrowed and became less well looked after. It was muddier and more overgrown. This time Humphrey took the main route through the gates.

He rode boldly and in broad daylight towards the manor. His approach caused a stir in the courtyard, dogs barked, men and women stopped their work temporarily to watch the dark clad stranger.

Humphrey continued on his way between the avenues of trees which led onto the courtyard. His mare's hooves clattered noisily on the stones of the yard as he entered. If he had not been noticed already, this clatter could hardly go unannounced.

He rode to the front of the manor house before stopping and slowly dismounting. A stable hand immediately came over to take the horse from the gentleman stranger. A servant came from the house to ask in what way he could help him.

"I have come to speak with your master, Meredith ap Howell ap Morris. I believe this is his residence." Humphrey confidently announced.

"He is indeed the master of this Manor." replied the servant. "Who should I announce has called to see him?" He enquired.

"Humphrey Kynaston of Myddle and Knockin." He announced confidently.

The servant seemed a little taken aback by this news and hesitated for a moment as he took a few extra seconds to look the stranger up and down. Having made his assessment he turned saying,

"Please wait here, while I tell the master of your request."

Humphrey was content to wait. He turned and surveyed the courtyard. His horse was being led across the courtyard towards the stables. The dogs had stopped their barking and had gone back to scavenging for scraps around the kitchen doorway. Workmen turned to go back to their various tasks, no longer diverted by the stranger's arrival. Unknown to Humphrey curtains twitched above him and eager eyes were silently watching him.

A few minutes later the servant returned.

"Please follow me, Sir. The master will see you now."

"Thank you." Humphrey was led into the house through the main doors. He mused to himself that this was not his usual entrance. He looked around at the grand entrance hall. His cloak was taken by another servant waiting inside the door. Humphrey was led to the main reception room, where the merchant, grey-haired, plump and covered in whiskers stood in front of the grand fire place.

"I recall meeting you on less agreeable terms Humphrey Kynaston. For what honour do I have for this visit? Do you intend to relieve me of my money, again?" The merchant came straight to the point. "If that is your intention, you will not escape on this occasion."

"I can assure you, Sir, that is not my intention." Humphrey replied calmly, "For our previous meeting you have my deepest apologies. Please accept this as a token of my apology." He produced a money pouch, which he laid on the table beside him.

"I will come directly to the main point of my visit, if it pleases you, Sir." Humphrey continued. The merchant nodded walking over and picking up the pouch. He opened it and his eyes opened even wider as he began to count the contents.

"I hope that will cover the previous amount plus some interest for the trouble." Humphrey added. "But I will come to the main point. As you no doubt are aware, I have recently returned from France in the service of the King. For that I have been duly rewarded by the return of my father's estates plus a not insubstantial financial stipend. But more important to myself and my brother, we have been granted a pardon for our past misdeeds by King Henry himself."

He paused and the merchant nodded, "Yes, I am aware of all this. How is this important to me?"

"Before I parted from England I had fallen in love with your daughter, Isabella. And I believe that the feeling was mutual. Now that I have returned in honour and wealth I seek your permission for her hand in marriage." Humphrey stood calm and confident.

The merchant stood in shock.

"Remove yourself from my house at once and never return. You are not welcome here. You may have a pardon in the Kings eyes. But you are known here as a common outlaw. You cannot change so easily. Leave at once and do not return. I do not wish to hear anymore of this preposterous idea. Good day to you, Sir. Fetch this gentleman's coat! He is leaving." The merchant bellowed to his servant.

Humphrey calmly turned around, collected his cloak and walked steadily through the hallway towards the door. From the stairway could be heard female voices. Humphrey turned and looked up. At the top of the stairs stood Isabella and her mother. Isabella gasped as she looked upon her secret lover. She did not know what to say or do.

"Good day to you, Madam and to you Isabella. Your father will explain my intentions, I am sure. I look forward to our next meeting." Humphrey confidently announced.

"There will be no next meeting, Kynaston. Leave immediately!" Bellowed Isabella's father.

"As you wish, Sir." Humphrey bowed to Isabella and her mother before striding out of the grand doorway. His horse was being led across the courtyard. She neighed as she saw him. He patted her neck and mounted easily. Again the curtains twitched from above the doorway. This time Humphrey looked up and saw his beloved Isabella looking down upon him. He blew her a kiss and waved. She responded beaming from the window. Humphrey turned his mount and rode away steadily and dignified.

Behind him he could hear the beginnings of the excited and emotional explanations and arguments that would go on for many days and nights within the manor house.

Over the next few weeks Humphrey sent flowers for Isabella and her mother, wine for her father and letters emphasizing that his intentions were honourable and that he wished to marry Isabella. He was now a reformed man, indeed pardoned by the King himself, and had honour and wealth for his part in the French wars.

The Merchant could not deny any of this. His daughter pleaded with him to relent and the mother also took her side, pointing out that Humphrey Kynaston was once more a wealthy landowner and would indeed be a good catch for their daughter. Less tactfully she pointed out that Mytton was dead and could no longer be classed as a viable suitor.

Slowly both the emotional and financial arguments appeared to come together in the Merchant's mind. Following yet another of Humphrey's letters, the Merchant sent a reply, requesting his presence to discuss the matter.

Once again Humphrey and his trusty mare followed the road into Wales. They both knew the way well by now. Unbeknown to the merchant and his wife, Humphrey had resumed his night-time ventures and had been reunited with his beloved Isabella on a number of occasions over these weeks. He needed her to know of his intentions and did not trust her father to honestly pass on his messages.

By now the dogs were used to him as a regular visitor and did not wake the residents of the household. As he rode up in daylight the dogs ran out but did not bark at this regular visitor, who usually had a few scraps for them. He threw them some of his left-overs as he approached and they were happy to see him. Isabella from her bedroom window was also very happy to see him. She watched him approach with excitement and anticipation.

He climbed down from his mare as previously and once again she was led away to the stables by a hand. Once again he was greeted by a servant, who went to announce his arrival to the master of the house. He was led through the ornate doorway, his cloak was taken by the servant and he was shown into the sitting room, where the merchant waited for him. On this occasion he was offered a brandy, which he gratefully accepted. The doors were once again closed. Both Isabella and her mother rushed down and tried to catch a word from inside, but to no avail. The doors were thick and the two men inside were talking softly and seriously. On this occasion there were no raised voices or bellowing. The discussions seemed to go on forever, so Isabella thought. At last they could hear movements approaching the door from inside, Isabella and her mother quickly scuttled back up the staircase to stand nonchalantly on the balcony.

The doors opened and both men were beaming.

"Bring Mr. Kynaston's cloak and have his horse made ready!" called the merchant in a good hearted manner. "I am glad that we have come to our agreement, Humphrey, and I look forward to our next meeting. You will come to supper on Sunday evening and the whole family will be able to meet you."

Humphrey shook his future father-in-law's hand. He took his cloak and looked up at the balcony.

"Good day to you ladies, I am looking forward to Sunday evening. Your father will no doubt explain to you our transactions of this day."

Isabella blushed and could not help herself giving Humphrey a little wave. He bowed to them gallantly before turning to go on his way. He rode away in triumph.

That night at the Wolf's Head there were huge celebrations with Humphrey standing the bill all night and well into the morning.

"How about one for the road, 'Umphrey?" Slurred an old friend. Humphrey turned to see Nancy advancing towards him.

Although he was very tempted Humphrey thought better of it on this occasion.

"I think I may have had my fill, Nancy. I feel I should now be on my way." He sidled off, not wishing to end up in the clutches of Nancy on this night.

"Please yourself. You usually do." She let out a raucous laugh.

"Well, perhaps times have changed." Humphrey spoke under his breath, so only he could hear his own thoughts. He slid towards the door and out into the fresh air, leaving the drunken revelry behind. He stood looking up at the stars in the clear autumn night. By the light of the clear moon he could make out the outline of the Nesscliffe, where for so many years he had made his home. He thought of the cave, where he and his horse had kept hidden from the Sheriff's men. It had been remarkably cosy. It was not the life he had been born into, but it was the one he had chosen. He had rebelled against the restrictions and expectations of his family and turned to the adventurous life upon the road, free from responsibility and care. But now he was getting older and he had truly fallen in love with someone he wished to live with for the years ahead.

His head began to clear as he breathed in the cold, fresh air and strode towards the stable, where he could hear the faint rustling and noises of the horses. He pushed open the heavy double doors of the stable and enjoyed for a moment the pleasant odour of warm straw and the smell of horse. His mare whinnied as once again she recognised her master.

"Hello, my love. I hope you have slept a little. I feel I need to pay a visit to some old haunts." He walked over and stroked her neck as she leaned towards him.

"That's my girl. Let's get you saddled up then, shall we?"

He collected the saddle from where it was hanging and saddled her up. Ten minutes later he was leading her out of the stables. Her hooves rattled on the stone yard as she was led across. Humphrey swung up into the saddle. He waved at the landlord, who now stood in the doorway of the inn, and trotted away.

He turned away from the highway and the pair began to climb uphill. The mare knew the route well, even though they had not passed that way for some time. The pair rode up to the base of the cave, where Humphrey had spent most of his years hiding out from the Sherriff of Shropshire. He dismounted and climbed the carved steps up to the entrance of the cave. He disappeared into the darkness. Gone was the fire he would have built, gone was the bedding over in the corner. It felt damp and bleak. He was hidden in the darkness of the cave for some time before he emerged. He quickly found his way down the steps despite the darkness. His feet seemed to remember the familiar crunch of the sandstone, worn smooth by his boots over the years.

He quickly reunited himself with his mare, effortlessly swung himself up into the saddle and began the downward journey through the trees and onward to his family estate.

He was to return once more for the last time many years later. He had lived a contented and fulfilling married life with the woman who had captured his heart. He had raised a family and had survived the turbulent years of King Henry's reign. Isabella had passed away a few years earlier and now Humphrey felt that his own time had come. He dismounted and unsaddled his horse. He waved her away as he slowly climbed the steps and once again disappeared into the darkness of the cave.

END